SWEAT

Also by Lesley Belleau

The Colour of Dried Bones
(Kegedonce Press, 2008)

SWEAT

by
Lesley Belleau

ScrivenerPress

Library and Archives Canada Cataloguing in Publication

Belleau, Lesley, 1976-, author
    Sweat / Lesley Belleau.

ISBN 978-1-896350-64-6 (pbk.)
    I. Title.

PS8553.E45698S94 2014   C813'.6   C2014-901612-3

Book design: Laurence Steven
Cover design: Chris Evans

Published by Scrivener Press
465 Loach's Road,
Sudbury, Ontario, Canada, P3E 2R2
info@yourscrivenerpress.com
www.scrivenerpress.com

We acknowledge the financial support of the Canada Council for the Arts and the Ontario Arts Council for our publishing activities.

For the mothers and children of Turtle Island,
and for all those voices that fill the future spaces.
G'zaagin. My heart is open to yours.

and she tumbled
& twirled
on her way
to a new world,
the dripping wet life
of her laughing
out loud
made aankwad (cloud)

"so this is what
it looks like,
around dusk
in spring!"

~Giizhigo Ikawe
on falling
and falling
again

in love.

~Waaseyaa'sin Christine Sy

Acknowledgements

THIS BOOK WAS WRITTEN WITH SUPPORT from the Canada
Council for the Arts and the Ontario Arts Council. I completed
this novel in the year between my third baby Tehya and fourth
baby Bianca. I would write in the spaces between playing with the
children, dinners, diapers, and breastfeeding. Chi-Miigwetch to
my four babies, Nicolas, Maddox, Tehya and Bianca who always
push me into that deeper place of creation.

I want to thank all of those who have encouraged my
writing and who pushed me to write from a perspective that
was my own. I appreciate the feedback that I have had from Dr.
Karl Jirgens and Dr. Bernie Harder at Algoma University and
University of Windsor. I would like to thank my family, my late
father, Wallace Belleau, mother, June Belleau, and sisters Becky
and Belinda who would read my stories when I was a little girl
and let me know they were valuable to them. This helped me

keep writing and remembering that love exists at the centre of all I do.

I acknowledge the missing and murdered Indigenous women and their families, and support the actions, writings and voices that emerge to create awareness of this horrific colonial injustice that endures still in this nation-state. May there be healing and justice and may our future generations be strengthened by our actions and words today.

Thank you to Scrivener Press, who honoured my desire to use Anishinaabemowin within my work and for the valuable editing and feedback through this process.

Miigwetch Christine Sy for offering your poem for use in this book. Your words are powerful and inspiring to me. Miigwetch also to Rosanna Deerchild, Cherie Dimaline, and Kim Roppolo for reading the manuscript and graciously offering comments for the cover. I am honoured.

Miigwetch to all those storytellers who placed stories in my spirit which continue to push forward my own life's creative force, helping me remember that we are all connected and that our memories and stories are ancient. We are continuing together, as women, as men, as ancestors, as writers, as mothers, as fathers, as activists, knowledge holders, and representative voices of places and times on Turtle Island where we welled up inside stories, filling up and pouring over, together. I am grateful to be a part of the big story that began so long ago.

A Story

THIS TREE WAS TOO BIG, LONGER THAN SHE CARED TO LOOK, higher than her squint could carry. It was blocking her view. Of what, she couldn't imagine, but it stood in the way of something, that must have been for sure. When her husband came home, she demanded that he rid of this tree.

"But, honey, it is much too large. I could never do this. It is a job much too large for me."

"Move it, or I must go. I cannot live here with that hideous tree blocking my view."

"View? Of what? There's nothing there!"

"I will not look at this for one more day." She paused, thinking, and then continued. "I will go picking some plants. I will return this evening, shortly after sundown. This tree must be gone, or I will not come in."

She turned and left.

Her husband walked round and round the tree. It was enormous. Gargantuous. Impossible to move. He went in and ate dinner, watching this tree. Impossible. He chewed and he swallowed, but no solution presented itself. He rather liked the tree. Its monstrous size kept him humble. He walked toward this tree and sat down, leaning against it. It felt good against his back. Warm. Sweaty. He felt its life through the bark. Felt its heat.

"Damned woman. Who does she think I am?"

The tree laughed.

"Who's there?" asked the man, worried, afraid.

The tree laughed again, this time, shaking its limbs, its strong back.

"Holy shit!" The man jumped to his feet, staring at the tree in horror.

The tree laughed harder at the man's pale cheeks, his shaking body. The tree laughed harder than it ever had before.

"What is so damned funny?" asked the man.

"You," said the tree.

"Me?" asked the man.

"Who else?" asked the tree.

"What? What? I just never heard a tree laugh is all."

"Well, you look pretty funny, all shaken up and shit. Never seen nothing like it."

"You wouldn't be laughing if you knew what I've been thinking."

"No? Well, fill me in."

"Been trying to figure out a way to get rid of you."

"Yeah, right. Good luck trying."

"No, really. The wife wants you gone. She wants to see in the distance, you know. What's behind you."

"Well, there's nothing there."

"Try convincing my wife of that. It's what she wants, that's all I gotta say."

"Your wife scares the shit outta me, brother."

"Me too."

They both sit in silent contemplation.

"When will she be back?" asked the tree.

"Soon, bro."

"I'm a little nervous, I have to admit," the tree stated, matter of fact.

"Don't worry, guy," the husband replied. "I have the axes all locked up in the shed."

"No, no. For you, dude. For you."

"Me? Yeah? Why's that?"

"Well, she comes back, say, and I'm still here, plain as day, what's she gonna do...to you?"

"Holy shit, you're right!" The husband jumped to his feet. "She'll be pissed for sure. Listen, what should I do?"

The husband paced round and round the tree.

"If you just would've asked, I would have moved," the tree stated.

"Really? You would?"

"Sure, why not? A change of view wouldn't hurt. I'm tired of looking at your brown ass every morning through your bedroom window. Little birthmark right on your..."

"Hey, fuck you. I'll be closing my blinds from now on..."

"But, I might miss your wife..."

"Hey! I thought she scared you."

"Sure," says the tree, "in a very sexy sort of way." The tree laughed lasciviously.

"Shut up, man."

"For real, your wife is hot. Especially when she wears those little red things … what do they call them … thongs? G-strings? You must know the ones I mean?"

"That's it, I'm leaving, you sick pile of bark. Imagine, watching us all this time. Got nothing better to do?"

"Naw, not really. Just the flowers to watch, the grass growing, and you two. And your wife, she is the best flower of them all. Full-grown. Mature. A ripe flower, spread open, revealing all her…"

"Shut up. Enough. Enough! Are you going to go or what?"

"I'll go. Sure. But you gotta promise me one thing," the tree said slowly.

"Anything. Anything. What's that?"

"If I go, you gotta deal with the consequences. Not my deal."

"Anything. Anything," the husband pleaded. "Please. You don't know what I'm in for if you stay."

"Alright, then." The tree shrugged, leaves falling all over the place. "Alright then. Nice to have known you."

The tree shifted, creaking slightly, roots straining, dirt lifting under the husband's feet. He fell, and the tree continued to shift and groan, and spread its limbs painfully. The ground came loose, the husband's eyes were covered in loose dirt, watering, spilling over his cheeks, up his nostrils, streams feeding, urging the ground onward.

Finally, the tree broke free. It carried itself away, not looking back, not saying goodbye, tree branches swaying, roots dragging over the hard, dried ground.

The husband sighed in relief.

Finally, the tree was gone, over the hilltop, all traces of its former existence vanished completely. Except for the gaping hole left behind. Except for the gaping hole that sat about twelve feet by twelve feet, the husband estimated, and was so obvious, and so, so much worse than the tree that once sat in its place.

"She'll freak out, blame me and I don't even want to think what else! This is awful, worse than that, horrible, unthinkable."

The husband paced the ground, peering into the blackness, weeping for his future, his bleak, sorrowful present.

He sensed her near and looked over the hill. There she was, basket in hand, whistling a happy tune under her breath. He started to grab at the twigs and leaves at his feet frantically and throw them over the dark, deep pit, the endless abyss, his head peering down into it, afraid of where it led to, unsure of the blackness, the dark eye that seemed to laugh at him, along with everything else. He turned to the south where she walked, looked up. He caught her eye, and waved at her. She waved back, looking for the tree, her long, black hair caught by the wind, never looking more beautiful. Breathless, he threw on more leaves with the one hand behind his back, his other hand waving to his love, desperate for her, longing to inhale her flower scents through her flesh.

He looked down. Finally, it was completed. A ground full of leaves to welcome his wife. Her beauty more rare than the fullest flower, her breath more potent than a thousand new births. He extended his arms and she began to run. She saw the tree was gone, she glided, thrilled, passionate, cheeks red, toward him. Her feet were bare, her dress pressed against her body. He saw her breasts through the fabric, full, perfected by time, nipples thrusting toward him. He could smell her, juniper, goldenrod, her milkweed thighs, and he almost brushed her brown fingers, stained green from picking stems, and he would have brushed those fingers, if she had not disappeared in front of his eyes.

Her scream filled the air, stopped all life around him, stilled the breath of all living things, all flying things, all growing things...

She fell through the leaves gracefully, her long, black hair above her arms, the tips of her fingers grasping wildly at the edge of the dirt, but missing, her mouth a perfect O, a beautiful centre. If she were a flower, her lips would be filled with ripe pollen at that moment, her perfect beauty revealed in her fall. He stared down the pit, pointed aimlessly down the deep abyss, saw nothing but the cold, cold air. He screamed her name: *Gheezhigo-Quae! Gheezigo-Quae!*

He never saw her again, just felt her in the movements below, in the quaking, the rushing of life, through the long, drawn out silences that pushed him toward the end of his being.

1

Beth

TREE LIMBS GNARLED OVER AND OVER each other like legs wrapped in love, wake her with their endlessness. This image stays through the morning, through the eggs and the clean-up, the sweeping outside the front door in case company comes. Tree limbs, long and graceful. Beautiful in their imperfections, like small leg-hairs, the new growth between beauty rituals, or the blond hairs that stay even when the black thick hairs are sloughed away blade after blade after blade. Limbs, wrapped together by time, hours upon years of their pressing together, bound by the dark air, the winters, the summer heats that work as glue, hard rainstorms like sweaty, needy love. Each birdchirp is a long pant between the sticky thrust of time, the tick of growth, formations of nest, a fresh revival over and over and over again.

She doesn't bother to wake him even though noontime passes. She leaves him resting in his own sweat, blankets furled around him, summer beating over him through the bedroom window. She does not draw the shades. She likes the edge of sun on his face. She likes the leak of his heat over the pillows, the damp odours, the strong scent of man in her bed. His breaths are long and slow. Makes her sleepy, makes her crave a fresh coffee. She likes to watch his wet sleep, and she sometimes pauses interestedly by the door, wondering about men and their dreams, thinking they must be dull, everyday sort of things, things that wouldn't catch her mind. She stays there by the entrance, leaning against the door-edging, loving this man while he sleeps, the small jumps of his fingers, his nervous eye-movements under his eyelids, the way the blankets hold him down, twisted around his body, so helpless while he sleeps, so lost to the world.

The phone rings and she walks down the hallway, watching the gleam of the ashwood floors, noticing a small scrapeline, and she bends to rub a long nail over it. *Could it be the kids, or him, or that dog that knows better than to come inside?* Somehow it never stays perfect, somehow, the dirt comes in, the tears, a bootmark, a mysterious scrape appears. But she could fix it with a filler, a polish, an oil. She will check the basement later for the solution. The phone stops ringing, but she walks toward it anyway, wondering if the coffee is still hot, feeling a slipping away, a sudden effort to keep from crying. She puts her forehead on the phone and bites her lip until she tastes the blood. She takes her head off the phone, and rubs the handle in case she left oil from her flesh on it, rubs, rubs, rubs until it is hot in her hand, shiny, the long wire wrapped around her hand, her arm twined with the wire roughly. Satisfied, she places the phone back on the hook, unwrapping her arm from the cord, over and over, the welty redness fading quickly against her bronzed skin, little slashes fading fast, as though never quite there.

Sweat

She can hear him restless on the bed. She knows that he is unrolling himself from his tangle of blankets, thrashing himself out of his mummification, his tight heat that has rushed him awake, created a need for release. She can picture him, spread-eagled, gasping for cool air, the heat lifting off his body, his long chest rising and falling, looking beautiful, soaked, sleepily discomforted, the curve of his lip, the scowl, the slow stretch out of a furnaced sleep. She turns away from the phone and goes to him, her body humming, a need building inside of her. She wants to feel the heat before he lets it go, wants to lie over him like a bearskin rug, retain the stifling air, sandwich it between them before the world steals it, before it hovers above them, leaving them cold, shivered, shriveled like dying grass.

2

Jolene

THE WATER CATCHES HER EYE through the trees and she stands
there, waiting for a tree to bend for her, to curtsey, to move aside,
to show her more. Nothing happens, just a quick birdwing in
the trees that might be her imagination, or a small sign of hope.
Everything seems too still out here in the bush, far from the city
sounds, from her friends screaming her name down the streets, far,
far, too far from anything recognizable. She stays where she is on
the picnic table, too scared to go inside, too intimidated to stay out
here. She is frozen, the sun beginning to slip lower in the sky, and
she feels like some weird growth, some new, ugly thing thrust out
in the wild; soon to be mocked by the others, the tree-bark, the
ferns, the long, broken cattails that seem to be something familiar,
from somewhere that she can suddenly taste, but cannot name.

A woman moves toward her. There is nothing for her to do but
to look at her. The woman has long hair, and looks like she belongs

here. Her long hair hangs low to her waist, she is sandaled, natural, scrubbed clean and pink-hued through the brown of her skin. She is beautiful in the bush, framed by trees and the water-edge behind her, made lush by this landscape. Jolene looks down, feeling guilty for being here, feeling eaten, nibbled at by this woman's arrival.

"Hi. Ahniin. Welcome sister. Is this your first time here?"

"Uh, yeah, can't you tell?"

"Of course not, I just haven't seen you or met you before. I'm Elsa."

"Yeah. Jolene. Came here by myself. Heard there was a sweat happening. You know, thought I'd check it out."

"Cool. Come on in. I'll introduce you to everyone."

She wants to hide, run to the bush, push this woman down and take someone's car from the parking lot and just drive to Toronto, to Sudbury, even just to Blind River for the night, anywhere, anywhere but right here, right now. They walk toward a huge wooden door, thick and smelling of heat and cedar. Jolene follows Elsa into the Healing Lodge and looks around. It is beautiful, larger than expected. Wood beams and doorways everywhere and smoke wafting from the center of the room. She smells something burning. What is that, tobacco? Sage? Sweetgrass? She can't decipher the various smells, it has been too long. There are about a dozen women inside, gathered. All the women are wearing long, flowing skirts, cotton, billowy and suddenly she feels stupid in her tight jeans and sparkly nail polish. They look at her and smile at her, but she knows that they are thinking the same thing: that she doesn't belong here, that she should just go home. She hangs her head down and tries not to look up too much when Elsa starts introducing her to the other women.

"Everyone, this is Jolene. She is joining us for our sweat tonight. It's her first time here."

All the women nod, or wave, or smile, but she knows they don't mean it, she knows they will watch her carefully, not trust her here in the middle of this place, where you can hear the water whisper strange things if you are quiet, where there are crickets in the grass, speaking, speaking, making you feel watchful, suddenly lonely.

Elsa motions for Jolene to take a seat on the edge of the wood base that surrounds a giant pit that is filled with small grey pebbles and stones with a large pile of burning wood in the center, the flames long and lean and crackling. She suddenly smells her childhood and her woodstove and feels both warm and cold at the same time, shivering, not sure if she should pull her sweater tighter or remove it. Jolene sits around the circle, sticking her feet in the scattered rock that lay at the bottom of the inner circle of the healing lodge, feeling hot again, but not wanting to take off her sweater where they will see her tattoos on her arms, the long scars down her shoulders. She decides to keep it on. She slips her feet out of her flip-flops and lets the rocks glide against her feet, enjoying the feel of her pebbles against her skin.

Elsa sits silently beside her, closing her eyes and leaning her head back as though asleep or dreaming or in deep thought. The other women sit as well, relaxing, not talking much and moving with the slow motions of the newly wakened. Jolene decides to try to relax and closes her eyes so she doesn't have to talk to anyone, make eye-contact or throw a fake smile across the room. She leans back onto her arms and keeps her eyes closed, feeling alone and stupid. She wonders why she came, and how she could leave without attracting too much attention. She wants to meet up with her girlfriends at Jimmy's party, where she should have gone in the first place. Now she'll have to wait, have to sweat it out. *Fuck it, fuck it, fuck it all.* She grits her teeth and hopes this all goes by fast.

3

The Grandmothers

ONE WOKE EARLY AND BEGAN A FIRE. She liked it so lonely that that she craved the sound of the water, the wind's fitful caress on her cheek. In tune with a breathing nearby, she broke twigs softly in her hands, snapping, snapping, snapping, each sound pivotal, each crack unique. Smokefire hair and she inhaled the dawn. Remnants of yesterday, everywhere. Fragments left behind, to take, to discard, to birth again, to destroy. She is a weaver. She builds from such piecings. Watches creation form from her fingers, the in, out, to and fro, from nothing, nothing, but unwanted pieces, pieces that don't make sense without the others.

Smoke lifted, formed into two dancers that flitted one around the other in a harmony that only morning can entice. Fancy dancers newly created from somewhere familiar, chins lifted, making this Grandmother laugh. She covered her mouth, not wanting to wake the others. Her feet began to move as she caught sight of the first flame, thanked the Creator for this new fire, and shifted her weight into dance, a dreamspace that opened for her, a piece of her quest revealed. Smoke lifted, her body drummed her toward a new day, and her fingers edged open, palms upward, thankful for the people, the use of this land, the long, long journey onward.

Sometime later, a dream came to her. In it, many birds were gathered, different kinds, various sizes, not one better than the other. It was dark and their species did not matter, only their voices. Some were strong, some were weak. Others opened their beaks and no sound came out. Some were silenced. Others opened their beaks and only long wails like childpains came out. Some were lost inside their wounds. Some could not take the sounds and left. Some began beating the wailing birds to silence them. Some began killing the wailing birds to silence them. Some went to sleep, unbothered. Others cried and preened their feathers in sorrow. Some did not notice and thought of how to get home. But some spoke firmly inside the noise to each other trying to be heard. Those birds recognized each other's voices and tried to move together, to gather closer, but everytime they shifted place, their bodies were pecked at in the dark, over and over and over.

This Grandmother ended her dance, brushing smoke from her eyes, out of her long wrinkles, out of her solid cheekflesh, her low earlobes, and moved aside. She knew it was time to wake the others, morning was surfacing and it was time to start the day. A baby cried from the circle of teepees, bodies shifted inside, a bird called out morning for the people to waken, let go of dreamtime, and rise toward daybreak.

The Grandmother began to laugh loudly for no particular reason at all.

4

Beth

SIMPLE AND VULNERABLE, THE WIND tastes newly formed, unfamiliar. This unnerves her, and she shivers, pulling her sweater tighter, watching the children play, sun beating over their flesh, beads of perspiration forming on temples, under the tight circle of their baseball caps. Construction hums nearby, a bird pierces through the playground, mothers look around, casual, relaxed.

"The world is too inaccessible," she thinks; "things so unattached to each other, nothing with connections, so distant."

She watches her children, remembers a show on kidnapping, how the predator will walk right into a park, like this one, and take the child right from under his mother's nose. The mother could be looking down, searching for a Kleenex, answering the cell phone and look up and her child could be gone. Just like that. As sudden as a sneeze, a daydream, a plane overhead. She will not take her eyes from her children, and silently scorns the other women as they chat together, casual, relaxed, like nothing could ever happen in a quiet city like Sault Ste. Marie. Well, things do happen, things can happen. Even in Sault Ste. Marie. Beth knows this as she watches her children dip in and out of the park's sandpit, casual and relaxed, unaware of their mother's eyes. She does not like construction so nearby, makes her nervous. She remembers living in Toronto, near Bloor West Village, and not far away, down on Bloor and Kipling, some construction worker hit a gasline, blowing up the neighbourhood. A hairdresser was cutting someone's hair, a tax centre blew open, a small apartment building shattered, probably with babies inside, maybe with an elderly woman admiring the day from her window.

She remembers the wife of the someone at the hairdresser's saying on the evening news, "It's my fault. I made him go out for a haircut. He really didn't need one, either. He looked fine the way he was. It's all my fault!"

So, Beth knows, things can happen fast, in the blink of an eye the whole world can change. Out of the corner of her eye, she sees a construction worker moving. She turns to examine him. He seems too young to be in the workforce, a teenager really. So young looking, so out of place with his hardhat and workboots and small hands beside the older, rougher men. She shakes her head. She hopes her boys don't go into construction. She wants their lives to be easy, simpler than a five a.m. wakeup, a bagged lunch, a few sweaty beers after work. More exciting than that. She notices that more construction workers are gathering together, staring down some huge hole dug in the street, pointing down the abyss. So many of them. A gathering of men. Some old, some young, some without shirts on, tattooed, dirty-nailed, and she knows why some women like these guys, like the catcalls, like the attention that a mob of men draws when a lone woman walks by.

She remembers the feeling of being on the spot, walking down the street past the construction workers, the knowing what is coming, a nervousness to look at so many men banded together. Tensing when they stop their movements to turn around and look, her skin burning, her eyes watering slightly from the attention. Why does she pull her tummy in, tilt her head just slightly, glad she wore her tighter shorts walking? She was disgusted by her own reactions. Who gave a shit if these guys notice that her waist is almost as slim as it was as a teenager? What if they stopped looking? So what? Then what? So.

Her head snaps from the construction workers back to the kids. She realizes just how long she was looking away, how easily she drifts. Anything could have happened. Anything. She is worse than the casual women that she was watching. A distracted woman is worse. Much worse. But the twins are fine, digging a deep pit in the sand, both of them looking into the hole, pointing down the abyss, quiet, reflective, two heads pressed together, identical, exactly the same. One dark-skinned, one paler than the stretched skin between her thumb and pointer finger. She is relieved and promises herself not to take her eyes from their bodies, hands caked with dirt, their open faces with the air receiving their skins.

Beth watches her boys, and thinks of yesterday. The cool breeze, swarm of words in her living room. She hopes she can be alone today. Thirteen of them in her living room. Artists, professors, writers, who knows who else. She baked for three days beforehand. Squares, puffs, brownies, butter tarts and a long roll of homemade bread for her arrangement of dips. They ate casually, leaving half-eaten pieces on her red ceramic plates which she later scraped heartily into the garbage can, thinking of the hours of baking, measuring, sorting, skills that did not come to her naturally. They talked, discussed her art, her latest show at the Art

Gallery of Algoma] and some of them pre-ordered pieces that she had created. They gathered around her long, planked harvest table in her dining room, observing the prints she had made of her new pieces, the flows of reds and blues and Ojibway colours blending into black. They asked her questions about Indigenous people, the inspiration she gets from her environment and nature and her reserve. She nodded, agreed, discussed pieces of herself, feeling like a traitor, feeling uncomfortable and violated, leaving fragments of herself laid out on the table with no discretion, without shame. She felt extirpated from her skin in her silk blouse and creased pants, a foreigner, a fake. No one seemed to notice the shake of her hand as she sipped her wine, hearty gulps that made her dizzy. When they left, Beth leaned against the door, relieved and exhausted, angry at herself for agreeing to this, furious for not being able to be the kind of woman that naturally falls into such a role.

She hated hosting. Felt false, pretentious. Heard her words, the lilt that wasn't her. A nod, a slow sip of wine. The cold sweat under her collar. She would rather be alone in the house. Sometimes when the doorbell rings she leans against a wall so that even her shadow doesn't show, plays a game with the kids.

"Shhhh...let's pretend we're not home. Shhh...duck. Let's pretend."

And she huddles with the kids against the wall, still, silent. The kids hold in giggles. She holds her breath, afraid. Afraid of what? Company? Ridiculous. But she can taste the blood in her mouth from biting her lip. But she can feel her heart pound. She must be crazy. She is sure of this. The listen for the walk away. The relief. The not caring who is there, knocking, ringing the bell. *Can't they just call first? So I look presentable, so the house is at least neat? So I can have some say if I want company or not? Is this normal to want this?* Afterwards, the quiet seems precious. She loves the smell of silence, the first supple scent, the drift in, falling leaves or lakewater nudges.

Beth retrieves herself from her thoughts and looks up to see they sky filling with dark-edged clouds, so swift, so seething. The other mothers race around, frantic, hair flying, gathering their children to their breasts, setting babies in strollers, zipping sweaters before the storm sets in. There is a scurrying of feet, a pounding against the dirt that sounds like dogs running down the long trail behind her childhood house. She takes her time, calling her children quietly, watching their small bodies respond, stand up and smile toward her. *Aww Mama, wait a few more minutes. Puh-lease!?* She almost consents, but realizes that the storm is coming in faster, darker, more persistent than ever. She shakes her head no and they follow her slow walk out of the park toward home. The other mothers are gone as the rain starts hard against them, pattering on their exposed flesh, the heat of their faces. The construction crew packs up, their cigarette tips still burning somehow under the rain. Beth walks slower and lifts her face to the sky, the rain cleansing what she is feeling. The boys look at her and lift their faces too, laughing. They walk hand in hand, drenched, all the way home.

5

Jolene

ELSA LIFTED THE FLAP OF THE SWEAT lightly and it made a small noise like a slap of a mosquito. Jolene followed Elsa inside. It was darker than she thought. Different than she thought. She figured that a sweat was a bunch of tree leaves, branches made into a hut. But what did she know? The sweat was outside of the healing lodge, down below a small hill, a dip in the earth. There were skins and canvasses hung and twined into shaven logs that formed a rounded hut of sorts. It was beautiful: the skins had a buckskin quality to them and the smell was thick, musky and earthy. There were shoes scattered around the entrance to the sweatlodge and a hole on top where smoke poured out, reminding her of Algoma Steel down by the river, except this looked whiter and cleaner, cottony and soft. The women nodded to her as they entered. Some brought in hand-drums, some entered without speaking, some sang softly. Jolene felt nervous and out of place, but she went in anyway, stepping inside with trepidation, trying to look solemn and peaceful as she ran her sweaty palms down the side of her jeans.

The heat was more intense than she would have thought, than she could have imagined. It was dark, but Elsa grabbed her hand and nudged her down to a soft spot of fur and it was quite comfortable, comfy, and she heard Elsa sit down beside her.

She leaned over and whispered to Jolene, "Don't worry, we are all right here. It's dark, but your eyes adjust and then you'll start relaxing. Just listen to the music and your instincts and if you want to leave to cool down, feel free."

"Okay, thanks," Jolene whispered back.

She sat back and tried to relax, even tried to close her eyes, but she began seeing yellow spots. She opened her eyes and tried to see the shapes of the women inside the sweat. The darkness was so full, so complete that this was impossible. Jolene let herself drift to soothe the nervousness that she felt, leaned back and breathed deep and heard the jaggedness of her breathing and wondered if the other women heard as well. She opened her mouth wide like a yawn and tried to inhale deeply and after several tries she got a nice deep breath and this motion soothed her slightly, made her feel better. She felt strange to be back in Garden River, a place she thought she'd never come back to, no matter what.

This was her first time back to the reserve in seventeen years, since she was eleven years old, since her mama left that August. Morning. It was morning then. Beautiful morning, the day after the big rains. She remembers, because the cats didn't come home. They never did after a rain. They stayed hidden in the red-shredded shed out back, scared. So, that morning she was calling to her cats.

"If they come in the next five minutes, they can jump in Uncle's car with us. If not, they belong to the bush," Jolene's mother says.

"No, mama, wait for them. They'll come. They're just waiting for the rains to dry is all. Let's peek in the shed."

"Hurry right back. We've gotta go. The big city is waiting for us." She laughs as Jolene runs in the back to the shed.

The shed is wedged shut, filled with old scraps of furniture, tree branches, metal car parts. She pushes and pulls roughly, scared her mama will run off to Toronto without her and leave her here in the bush, alone.

"Shit on a stick," she whispers, not wanting anyone to hear her use bad words. "Shit on a stick of bricks."

The door will not budge.

She hears a cat's meow. A slight echo of a cat's call.

"Mittens? Issat you?" she hisses through the crack in the door.

"No," a voice rings out.

"What the heck?" Jolene spins around.

No one is there. Just the shed, the path to the water, and hordes and hordes of trees.

"Who's there?" Jolene whispers, frozen to the spot, blood pounding in her ears, a drumbeat, a slow stride.

"Relax, girl. Just trying to help you find your kitties."

"Who are you?" Jolene turns around. "Where are you?"

"Don't worry about it. Listen. One of your cats is stuck up that big oak tree to your left. Been there all morning. Too scared to come down."

Jolene looks up to see that whoever was speaking, is right. There is Mittens mewing up so high on that tree branch, unable able to come down.

"But...but where is Milkshake, the baby?" she asks the air, looking around.

"In the shed, too scared to come out without his mama."

Jolene speaks loudly. "Like you? Too scared to come out, like you?"

Sweat

There is a long, low laugh. "I am out, Kwayzenhs."

"What-the-fuck-ever," Jolene mocks, then gets scared in case it is one of her momma's friends, listening to her swear.

"You got quite a mouth on you for a little girl," the voice laughs.

"Sure do, don't I?" Jolene twirls around. "Now come out, come out wherever you are and help me get my cat."

"Jolene!" her mother calls her from the front of the house. "Get your butt over here. We're leaving!"

"Wait Mama, for goodness sakes, wait!" Jolene shrieks.

"Are you sure she wouldn't leave without you?" the voice asks.

"Of course not. She's my mama."

Jolene tries to climb the tree, slips, blood runs down her leg.

"Come on out and help me get this goddamned cat!" She is angry now.

"You really want my help?" the voice asks.

"Yes, dammit, yes," Jolene shrieks into the dense forest. "Yes, yes. Please."

"Well, okay, now that you're being polite," the voice replies.

Without warning, a low rumble begins. Jolene looks around, terror filling her up. "What...what is that?" she whispers.

The rumbling spreads from the back of the trees to the front. Jolene wants to run, but she can't will her legs to move. The cat meows and the tree limbs start shaking, shaking, a sound that she's never heard before, a deep sound that she remembers from somewhere, a reverberation that smells earthy, fulfilled, and sharp, clear as the long, drawn out scream of birth. The cat tries to hold on, its claws flailing in the air, its mouth snapping open and closed. Jolene tastes spring in her mouth, rivers down her throat, and she is no longer afraid, just mesmerized by the scene in front of her, awed by the sight of her cat falling through the air, and landing on her feet in front of her.

33

The cat looks around, licks her paws and brushes herself against Jolene's legs. She meows and Jolene picks her up. "Mittens, you silly cat."

She looks around. "How the hell did you do that?"

There is no answer. The bush stares back at her. She feels challenged and she likes the feeling. Exhilaration, a bravado that she has never felt before. She places the mother cat by the shed door and moves forward, quickly, before she loses her nerve. She moves in and out of the trees where the voice came from looking around for somebody, prepared to see a neighbour, a helpful stranger, a friend of her mother's lounging there, back against a tree, chewing on a fern stem. Nobody. Twigs crack, her breath comes in short bursts, she twirls around, nervousness returning. She peers up trees, her eyes weave through the branches, searching helplessly for a face to connect with the voice.

She finally leans against a tree and immediately screams in pain at the heat emanating from it. An intense burn saturates her body with a sudden sweat, but she can't move. It is as though hands are holding her against the tree, pushing her against it. She feels the bark of the tree as flesh, has the sensation of being against a feverish body, breasts pressing into her back, a hardened stump twisting down her thighs; a memory of fingertips flailing, a slight cry that she remembers tasting like fear and comfort and the swelling of dreams that want to be remembered. She writhes in confusion, wondering who is on the other side of the tree, starting to panic. Until she hears the voice beside her ear, swathed in aging birch bark and what she imagines the inside of acorns would smell like.

"Don't I get a thank you, a quick migwetch?"

"Thank you, thank you. Now let me go."

The hold loosens and she runs, not looking back, both cats following her closely. She scurries into the backseat of the car and watches as the cats hop onto the mats on the floorboards. She locks both doors and watches her mother slide in slowly.

"About time Jolene. I almost left without you."

They pull out of the reserve in silence, not speaking, not planning on ever coming back.

But here she was. Jolene closed her eyes in the sweat, nervous, panicky, wanting to push through the women and crawl out and crawl far away where no one would ever see her again.

6

The Grandmothers

THIS ONE REMEMBERED HER DESCENT. It was springtime, a warm evening. The people were either preparing an evening meal or relaxing, watching the children play. Sometimes the boys chased each other in hunt, the girls wove baskets, ignoring them, or made dolls with blades of grass and straw and rods, twirling the pieces round and round and round. She fell in the dusklight, her long hair flying upward, body long and brown, fell between skybreak and the wateredging, fell. This one remembered her descent, long and full, the spiritworld laughing out loud into the night.

Somehow no one else noticed, just this one and all of the animals watching in the bush around her. They came out when she landed. Stood beside the grandmother, brushed against her legs. Foxes, raccoons, wolverines, coyotes, and behind them all, the muskrat, watching, watching, small eyes bright in the dusk. From the water, the otters watched, the beavers and all of the fish of the deep. The grass where she fell was browned, flattened, hard as the outer shell on a turtle's back.

. The old woman walked forward to see the younger woman. She lay there, sprawled on the sunbaked grass, sleeping. She was beautiful, full inside of her womanhood, her long, black hair waistlength, spread over the grass, mingling with the earthnoises. Her face was serene, a half-smile on her lips. Black lashes closed over her eyes. Her body was long and lean and full. Breasts falling to one side, nipples brown and hard-tipped. Her legs were strong and long, reminding the woman of a deer in mid-hunt. Between her legs, pink flesh lay open wide, tissue upon tissue, a clear liquid edging out, slight trails of womanblood still visible. A ladybug trailed her cheek, but the woman did not stir.

The old woman breathed out, astounded by the lushness of the woman that lay before her. She was all women, exploding. Breathing in, the old woman smelled love in all stages, birth emerging and the first drip of water toward the earth in rainfall. She heard a child cry out from the flesh of the young woman, heard a groan of love at midnight, heard the final expulsion of breath from a dying grandmother, and the old woman wept for her women, for the women to come. She kneeled near the flesh of the young fallen woman and wept longingly and bitterly. She reached out a hand and dipped her finger in the womanblood on the woman's thigh. She lifted it to her lips and cried out at its taste. It tasted of steel and pain and love and joy and birth and death and life and dream and thought combined, and she cried out. She absorbed the flavour into her tongue and cried out for the women to come, tears falling on the one who fell. The fallen woman awoke and sat up, clutching the arm of the grandmother. She did not wonder where she was or how she got there. She cried out with the woman, wept with her, and drew strength with her for the years to come.

7

Beth

THE TWINS WATCH BETH, NEITHER ONE BLINKING, neither one giving a hint what they want from her. She is confused, wondering what was said before the lead-up to this point. They both stand there, their faces identical, every feature exact, so much so that it is startling, frightening at times. They seem to blink at the same time, shift their weight evenly, glance sideways at each other so precisely that she is mesmerized, as though she is watching the creation of a choreography so finely that she should be recording this moment with a videocamera instead of her eyes and mind. The only difference is their hair. One's hair is the darkest black, the other's is the purest blond.

She feels she must speak.

"Okay. What is it? What do you two want?"

"Mommy, you weren't even listening again!" Keith screams, his hands running up the side of his face and squeezing his blond hair.

Sweat

"Mommy, really. This is pretty important," Juno says, hanging his head.

She feels guilty, off-centered, confused. What just happened? A fight, a dispute over plastic dinosaurs, marbles? What? What?

"What is it guys? What is it? For goodness sakes, keep it down."

"Mommy, we missed our soccer game again!" Keith shouts, his cheeks red, scalp red under his blond hair. "Daddy's working late again and you just forgot. You just forgot about our game!"

"Oh shoot, oh shoot. What time is it?"

"Half an hour too late, that's what time it is!" Keith yells, throwing a plastic stegosaurus at her, running from the room.

It bounces off her leg and lands on the ground with a thud. She looks at Juno and he runs into her arms.

"I'm sorry, sweetie. So sorry. You know, I just went into my studio this afternoon for half an hour and I started painting and I lost track of time…" She feels tears in her eyes and wonders about her emotions lately.

"It's okay mommy, but Keith really wanted to play. Well, me too, but it's okay. What did you paint? Can I see?"

She looks at him, his black hair over his left eye, and lets her heart edge toward him, cover him, drip all over him.

"Yes, baby. You can see."

They begin to walk toward her studio, passing the bedroom hallway on the way toward the end of the long hall.

They listen at Keith's door, knock, and hear him yell. "Beat it. Just beat it."

She shrugs at Juno sadly and they finish the walk together to her studio. Inside, sit dozens of canvases. Some finished, some not. Juno loves to run his fingers over the sides of the canvas, loving the rough, but smooth feel, the bare heat from his fingers. He loves the colours she uses, deep swirls, reds and yellows dipped into each other.

"What is this one called?" Juno asks Beth in excitement.

"Corn," she tells him.

"Corn?"

"Yes, honey. Corn was very important to the Ojibwe people. That's what we are. Anishinaabe."

"Corn people?"

"Yes. Corny Anishinaabe people..."

"You're kidding."

"Am I?"

She chases him around with the canvas over her head, snorting and hissing. He runs, laughing, black hair glinting like midnight, his eyes bright as starlight, his laugh newness and moonlight spread as a wingspan over water. They stop and he looks serious, watching his mama.

"I'll go talk to my brother," Juno says.

"Please, honey. Tell him I'm sorry." Beth looks nervously down the hall, where her other, angrier boy sits in his room.

She watches Juno go, so small still, six years old, shoulders slumped slightly with apprehension. He looks back. They both smile. She turns toward a new canvas, puts it on a sturdy frame and opens her palette. Flashes of her quiet son burst over her senses. Smile so wide, spreading always, pushing his cheeks apart so easily, little teeth like smooth white stones, hands are starfish cascading, blooming constant creation. Juno with his brown eyes so brown they seem black until the naakshig comes, a true nightsky, and then one can see them, nothing but brownness and inside of their mystery slivers and crevices of oranges, chestnuts, hazelnuts falling onto an earth carpet running into autumn skies. Juno with his laughter that curves like moons, pulls others into a sound so familiar and magic that he is often surrounded, and she paints her son, his cycles of wonder, his curved eyelids, a night spirit, his voice and laughter until she sees only him in all of his glory held by her hand. Beth paints the colour of his love until her arms are sore, until the nightglow falls over her arms through the window and she turns, alarmed, wondering where time goes, how it disappears on her without warning.

Beth puts down her brushes, wipes the edges of her fingertips on her apron, her eyes sore, arms aching. She rinses her brushes quickly, efficiently, worried about the time, the children, wondering about her husband. Peeking at her watch, she sees it is past nine and she scurries out of her studio.

She goes to her room, peeks in at the kids, sleeping, their beds identical, their room perfectly symmetrical, everything balanced, everything silent, and she is guilty for painting instead of seeing her sons to bed, wondering if they are angry at her for not coming, thinking that they probably forgot to brush their teeth. She vows never to do this again, to wait until they are asleep before she gives in to her urges for art. Ashamed and sorrowful, she walks slowly to her room at the end of the hallway. She is guilty for her awkward mothering which never seems right no matter what she does. She wonders how she can make up for this tomorrow, what she can do to make tomorrow erase today. *Does she deserve to be a mother? Did she deserve these children?* She doesn't know what she'd do without them. She really doesn't.

Beth enters her room. Her husband sleeps. His shoes are still on, hair still perfect, looking impeccable. He is beautiful, softer in the moonlight, his chest, with its slight rise and fall, the perfect buttons lined down his chest. She did not even know he was home. Did he come into the studio? Did he say goodnight? She doesn't remember, and feels horrible for not noticing, not putting supper out. How did she forget? Why can't she prioritize properly? She slips off her sweater, her paint-stained sweats and slips a nightie over her head. She brushes her teeth and washes her face. She turns toward her husband and sits on the edge of their bed. She is not tired, does not feel like bathing or painting; just sitting here watching her husband sleep is enough for her. His face is art, his cheeks indented drastically, his teeth the colour of shaved wood in the half-light, his lips full, moist. She touches his face, rubs the bristle with her palm, leans in and smells his cologne, the slight edge of brandy on his breath. She's sure that she loves him. She must. She must. *She must.*

She slips his shoes off, examines his perfectly clean socks, his lack of scent. But she senses his heat, and she shivers. Crawling under the blankets, she curls into him, nuzzling his neck, trying to pour a love into him that he will accept. She presses against him, trying to share his heat. The sleeping is difficult, the falling into it impossible. She wills it for minutes and half-hours and hours and big blocks of blackness. She tosses and turns, her black hair cold. She wants him to wake, for him to turn to her and lift himself into her, plunging into her from behind so she can flail blindly, not seeing him, not having to read him with her eyes, examine him, so she can simply press against him, taking him in, forcing herself onto him over and over until he falls over her exhausted, and she doesn't have to think about anything else.

But she knows he will not wake. She knows that he will be gone when she opens her eyes. And she won't have to worry about afterwards, when the sex ends and she rolls over to him, wondering why he doesn't seem familiar, why she feels like an adulteress, a whore, like she just screwed a perfect stranger that she only met minutes ago. She tries to forget these things and she closes her eyes, pictures of handprints and nightskies and the whole world exploding behind her lids. She grows afraid and thinks about paint and the way that the colours blend into each other so easily, so casually, and how the new colour always seems right and perfect and she sees her hand over a long row of colours, dipping and swirling and creating a shade that will satisfy the whole world through.

8

Jolene

So hot and thick her throat constricted. Jolene gulped down the heat, feeling it enter her trachea, lungs, belly. She tried to breathe evenly and deeply so she wouldn't panic. She heard Elsa humming beside her, but didn't know who the woman was that she had sat beside; she hadn't known it would be so fucking hot. She decided to squeeze her own leg to make sure that she was still here. She felt dizzy, wanted to crawl out quickly. She squeezed harder, resisted the urge to pinch the thigh of the woman beside her. It was so black that her eyes roved everywhere to find a pin of light. She just wanted one glimpse of light so she'd know she still existed. The black was so intense that she concentrated on her breathing to fight the full fear that was starting to choke her. She wanted noise. She wanted fire. She wanted out.

Some women began to sing softly. It was something and her panic gave way to a thickened awareness, one filled with the feel of her flesh under her hand, the rise and fall of her chest, the deep drum of her heartbeat. She waited to hear a quickening of her heart, but it remained calm, and she started to relax slightly with the in-out movements of her breathing, with the soft Indian words that crept into her from a strange woman's voice from somewhere out of the space. She drifted for long minutes, catching new scents of recollection, some from a childhood dream, some from her gut, pulled out in quick succession.

"Remember honey, always have a backup plan in case your first one don't work out." She hears her mama's voice, loud and clear, and she jumped slightly, wondering if anyone else heard or if the heat was making her doze off and hear things that couldn't be here.

"I know mama, but my plans will work out, I know they will." She looks at her mama and her mama looks back, not blinking.

She thinks of that day; the way the snowdrifts rise over the house, making the whole world seem brighter, hidden. Just her and mama, just how she likes it. Cinnamon toast mornings, a twang of the guitar at midnights, the smoke, the low laughing, the way her mama sees her and smiles that slow smile, surprised always by the dimples she always forgets that mama has until she smiles those slow smiles.

"Listen, mama, let's play that I'm the Bugwayshinini and you are home alone and you see me outside the front window while you're making coffee. Let's pretend that."

And they do. Mama screeches when she sees the "Sasquatch" out the window, a long, dutiful screech, her black hair flying over her eyes, the tearing of the cheeks with her long nails, a stagger backwards, a slow run to the bathroom to lock herself in. And she runs at mama with lunging, menacing steps, busting through the front door, and groping at the bathroom door. Mama almost has it locked, she pushes through harder and harder and mama isn't up for the fight, she collapses on the floor, hands over her face and she screeches and screeches as it bears down on her and Jolene hesitates because the scream seems so real and Jolene hesitates because her mama screams so loud and hard that she feels scared for her and Jolene reaches down to her mama's cheek and rubs her, helps her to her feet and says, "Mama, mama. I'm sorry."

"Honey, honey, I'm just pretending. You said that didn't you?" Her mother looks worried.

"I know, I know. I just don't like the game anymore."

"Okay, that's okay. Let's have a tea and sugar and jam crackers."

"Yeah, okay."

And Jolene watchs her mama walk away to make the tea, her thin back to her, and she calms her beating heart, not knowing why she got scared, not knowing why she had a sick pit in the deep of her stomach. She just feels the edge of her childhood scraping raw against the snowy window, feels suddenly warned, icy, and desperate for her mother's eyes on her, not looking away, not wavering, but steady, fierce.

But she does not look at her once. Jolene waits, unable to speak, but her mother scurries quickly across the kitchen, humming, drumming with her feet, not noticing her daughter, pale against the bathroom door, fighting for her breath, for a full gulp, her hands kneading her thighs, her eyes never leaving the woman with the long hair that made her fear her future, who drove kisinaa through her veins without saying a word.

Jolene was surprised by her tears on her face. She lifted a hand in the darkness and the tears were hot against her already enflamed flesh. She wondered quickly if she was being loud and sniffly, if the other women heard. She didn't know, and they continued to sing. She heard a drumbeat inside the sweat, and she realized that someone must have brought a hand drum in. She liked the beat of it, the way it carried her mind away from here into somewhere else, a further place than dream, and where memory was peeled open like a fine skin, layer by layer.

But this time, just voices. A place where faces don't exist, a place where flesh is a costume, a guise. She has never been here before, this place of whispers, echoed laughter, a deep wail from far off. She feels her senses turn this way and that, bend, roll over each other gracefully like otters. Her tears don't exist here, but she can understand their heat, can recognize the smell of their heaviness, like a sudden fog before dawn, filled with movements the earth watches outside the curve of moon. Those dark shapes that our stomachs sense, those little nudges, the smears at the corner of our vision. She pushes herself away from them, recognizes their disdain towards her, the protracted smiles by their sides, the pulse of energy surrounding them like sentinels. She isn't frightened, just curious how she couldn't have known this before. Everything seems so familiar, she thinks, so obvious. She feels propelled toward a deep static, a vibrating undertone that she feels is pulling at her, yanking an obscure cord. It does not seem possible that she knows this sound, but somewhere within her, there is a resonant flicker of memory, a rush in and out of taste and sudden sentience. She is overcome with the salt from the sea, a wave of nausea, love, a dampened misery wrapped in a tight fist carving itself gently into the cusp of her heart. Small indentations begin and she is seven, alive inside the sea, tasting the salt on her cheeks, her tongue a tadpole rotating around and around and around. Her mama's voice calls out to her.

"Over here. Just walk forward, right into my arms."

"Okay mama, but I have water in my eyes. I can't see."

"Just walk. I'm right here. Right here, baby."

"Okay mama. Okay then."

The wave hits hard, knocking her small body over. She opens her eyes and they sting, are slapped with more water, her nose fills, lungs suddenly open, gasping for air, but taking in rushes and rushes of water. There is blue-black behind her eyes, a knocking, the gurgle of voices so far away, and her legs kick out, trying to force the power of the onslaught back, but she trips herself, falling under, her hand gets caught in her hair, and she feels it get trapped in her hand, her scalp being pulled at, forced from her skin. *Mama,* she thinks, *Mama, where are you?*

She is back to a voice that travels like a curved creek, the simple whisper of one who is used to being alone. One who does not need the company, but will accept it if it presents itself. It is so close, almost reaching to the core of what she is. *Zhaashkoonh.* It is not a man, nor a woman either. It is the sound of creation. The singular imprint of a first cry. A drip of blood on a freshly dried sheet. A small paw digging its way into ancient soil.

"You have come," the voice says.

Jolene won't respond until she can understand how she feels about this voice. She needs to know more. She hesitates.

"That's alright," it says. "I felt the same way, first time."

"First time what?" Jolene decides to ask, the threat of knowing less important than her curiosity.

"First time breathing. That's all. Your first breath, the suck in, sharp as fear, necessary as the swell of love."

"I'm sorry, I don't understand. This is my first time here."

"Yes, I know. Good to see you again."

Jolene feels something pull back from the voice. She understands suddenly the colour of flight, not dark or light, or any shade she'd ever seen, just as fast as the formation of speech, the slow circles of an eagle's mission, a glimpse of the furthest rock, shifting, a baby's first gasp of air. She smells a fragrance. Cedar? Sage?

But it's not that, it's something else. Something here seems permanent to her, a concrete-edged scrutiny the seconds before the final lunge, the brisk walk, the full-fledged run. And the thing that is left behind. That is what is holding her, speaking with a casual ease, a knowing grasp. The thing that thinks it has her, she thinks. Talons, tips breaking into mouseskin, blood-tipped, sharpened against rock and bark, regrown when pulled out, replenished over and over again until the death where the final claw lay, dulled down by time, withdrawn into itself, useless at last.

Jolene laughs here. And screams. Breathes her voice into the other. It doesn't speak back to her, just observes her with its silence. Watching her spectacle of sound. Her pants that turn purple, swell into bruises before her eyes, purple lines that wriggle wormy away from her. She uses her voice to try to scare this thing. Make her sound a claw, but it doesn't move under her resonations, the gutteral squawks that she pushes out with her core, reddening before it, exhaling with all her might, and then she stops and accepts the silence. And the rage is gone. The other voice dissipates, as though bored, or satiated. The edges around her voice fall off, tiny slabs hitting a wet surface beneath her, a hollowed stump, and she marvels at the sense of this place, at the ease at which things are tucked away, the neatness inside of swirls of movement; but for a minute it makes sense and she joins the memory of laughter, joins it with all her strength and song.

Mama, mama, where are you?

And when she rises from the water, her mother is screaming her name: *Jolene! My girl! Jolene! Jolene!*

And Jolene steps toward her, legs shaky, throwing up water, a soft splash as liquid connects with liquid. *Mama, Mama.*

And her mama turns, mascara down her sloping cheeks, long black hair limp and damp, a look of horror on her face, relief and horror until Jolene looks down. Her mother's arms around her, carrying her back to shore.

Somehow, the drumbeat continued and she was back in this place, as though thrown overboard. She laughed still, soaking with sweat, the drummers never ceasing, their voices, underwater, so far, far away.

9

The Grandmothers

THE GIRL HUNCHED FORWARD WITH ALL HER MIGHT and the Grandmother thought she might topple. Her belly loomed large out the front of her naked body, the writhe of a ready child shifting visibly. Her legs had long veins, purpled under her brown flesh. Her breasts were massive, nipples stretched wide and tight over her flesh. Bellybutton shifted back and forth above the baby's movements. The girl wailed from her gut, pushing her breath out in harsh thrusts, reddening from the neck up, gripping the Grandmother's arm as hard as she could.

Leather, the girl thinks wildly, her arm is like leather.

The Grandmother soothed the girl, so young. The fear in her eyes, the panic that a first birth brings.

"Hush, little one," the Grandmother sang, half-words, half-music.

The girl fell to her knees, pounding at the ground. Clawing at the dirt like a bull, wanting to tear her hair out, screaming life and death at the woman whose hand was entering her body, shifting something clockwise. The pain could not be comprehended. There must be something wrong. Her insides were twisted together so violently that she was sure of death as the liquid pours out of her. Who was this woman with the beads around her neck, strumming this agony so calmly, trickles of sweat near her low ears, falling into long strands of graying hair? Where did she come from? Who sent her?

A searing heat opened her wider, the Grandmother moved faster, stretched the girl open gently, using her fingers to enlarge the tissue, pull it wider with patience so the tearing didn't come. Labia, the round red moonness, her face screaming, pulling the pulling the pulling the pulling, a departing. Body lifting to that space. That breath an animal, panting life in bursts out of her nose, blood over her lips, down her throat, pouring out from her nostrils. Her eyes were fire, burning from the inside out, seeing her lover's face before ejaculation, turned away from her, teeth bared, spittle forming at the corners of his mouth. His short movements before his low moan, his falling, his head on her chest, his sweat absorbed into her body, her pores, her blood, her histories. She loved him, his soft hair in her mouth as she sucked it, wanting to swallow it, all of him. Her body prayed for his baby, used her fingers to hold his liquid in, raised her hips as she watched his eyelashes against her neck-skin, held him close as she whispered to him.

I love you, I love you, I love you. Gi zah gin. Gi zah gin. Gi zah gin.

The Grandmother rose, crying softly, smiling, and prayed over a large bowl of water.

"This water is sacred," she told the girl.

The fire licked the girl's thighs, her mind, cast strange lights behind her pupils. The girl saw water rising over the windows of this cabin, she saw trees with faces, some with kind eyes, some laughing maliciously, some crying for her, their barks turning soggy and floating away like paper upstream.

"Push now," said the Grandmother. "Gentle now, I can see the top of his head. You need to slow down, dear one. You need to look in my eyes. *Oskenzhig.*"

She did and saw a thousand babies in birth, pink bodies immersed in bloodied streams, faces scrunched tightly, fists in motion, swimming upstream, rushing over rocks, waterfalls, the lifeblood, toward the beat of their mother's heart. She bore down, her teeth releasing blood under her lips, the blood over her breasts, smearing into her pores, her histories, a darkness that lay in wait inside of her. Afraid, she was breathless, wondered what the taste of death was, how dank it was, if it was anything at all like the morning her mama left and the months of waiting afterwards, the cold windows that her fingers traced, the woodpile that did not last the winter, the driveway that piled thick with snow with no one to know she lived on behind it. The taste of baked beans and smushed peas and alphagettis mashed into one. The sound of footsteps in the spring to take her to the foster home, a new mother with her green eyes that had never left her back since then, who hissed at her from corners, a slow, careful snake, thick with muscle, as long as childhood. The wish that she had hidden from the knocking, fallen back from the shadows, her breath still, pretending that she didn't exist. A long scream sounding like thirst and earth rolling out of her.

The baby's head emerged. Black hair jutting out of her pink labia, her bloodstained thighs. Women's fingertips slipping inside of her, pulling her open, wider. The Grandmother laughed at the hair, telling the girl that all her children had the same thick, Ojibway hair. This calmed the girl, convinced her that she was not birthing a monster, a freak; that this was normal, not an animal or creature edging out of her body. The Grandmother rubbed herbs on her legs, massaged the girl's thighs, edged her open further, slowly and with more love than she knew how to accept; the girl watched the old woman, her old mouth smiling, tears running down her cheeks in springtime melting.

"Here he comes," she whispered.

And the girl opened her eyes with the shriek, with her son's first wail of life.

10

Beth

FEELING URGED ON BY SOMETHING, SHE PAINTS. Sometimes the colours swirl outward, her hand an instrument for the artist behind her. She feels taken over and alert and powerful at the same time. She wants weeks of sleeplessness, months of being in the same studio, same smock, same ticking of the clock behind her with no disturbances. The boys will be home in two hours and supper is not thought of. Her husband did not call so she has no idea what his plans are or if he will arrive after midnight again, tiptoeing to bed, black leather shoes upturned by the front door, laces still tied tightly. The canvas edge is browning like burned kindling, a life emerging from the blur of her fingers. Somehow a tree is forming, knots delicately swirled into the trunk, the paints on her palette falling into each other, her breathing balanced, a rhythm against the ticking of the clock, an orchestra mingling with the air outside, the pulse of the ceiling light, a dim hum of a transport driving by.

Her hands feel alien to her, they always do. She is skinny, but her veins are thick and ropy over her hands and they look like the hands of an old lady in the sunlight. Fingernails bitten down, reddened by her toothends, scraped raw and red, the separation of skin and nail so clean and neat. But she loves her hands, the mysteries they make and the way that they move inside of this room.

The trees take shape on the canvas. The trunks grow long, shades of browns and blacks filtering in a pale dusk sun over the branches, her breathing a wind on the page, her fingers etching a history of life-rings and tiny nodules and bumps of bark that she inhales as her own. She feels the insects living inside the flesh of these trees, burrowing inside the grainy crevices, intersecting each other, making families, reproducing rapidly and piling up inside these trees, enduring. She senses roots under the ground, can smell their muskiness, feel their long limbs, supple and smooth, perfect for kneading. Her hands take on the shape of a carver's hands, ancient, melt into the sound of a quick and steady whittling, an energy of dance that is like mating. Her hands are quick, veins shifting under the movements of her fingers, wrists cramping slightly, and she is happy, feels something very close to joy as she watches the elongation of these trees taking shape, the newness of their forms, the smell of them filling the room. Husky earthmarks, the swirls like currents over the scratchy bark and slivers of woodgrain, and her hands mark the histories inside of the branches, each leaf, the trails of roots edging underground, a colony of ants disappearing underground.

She steps back hours later, exhausted, looking at the finished painting. Beth becomes mesmerized by the shaping of the two large trunks and is awed at their silhouettes which protrude like two pregnant women ready to birth. The stomachs of the trees bulge as though heavy with babies. She could almost see the shape of the infants that lie within. *Very strange*, she thinks. *This wasn't at all in my mind when I began.* She sees a knot on each trunk that look very much like a bellybutton straining against the flesh of the tree from the bulge of child within, stretched taut and firm and undeniably hard. She examines the two silhouettes with her trained eye, slightly disturbed and exhalted. She can almost see the shape of the woman leg on the side of the trunk resting below a curve of hip, swell of breast, even the soft nub of nipple. She can almost hear the infants shift and wonder what that feels like, a full-term baby stretching within the womb. She feels an ache in her belly, a thirst for something far off and can hear a cry of a baby from somewhere, echoing. Then she does hear a scream. A piercing cry and she feels off-balance, as though falling through space, an echo of wind in her ears, a siren of air rushing into her windpipe, through her chest and resting in her stomach, stretching it out, ballooning it outward and she crumbles, piling softly on the floor as though caught by strong arms, cotton, a long field, flat and dry.

"Mama, mama." She hears the voices coming closer.

"Mama, get up." A child's voice, worried.

"Keith, call daddy at work. Mama's sick. She's fainted." Juno's voice grows frantic. "Quick, find the number. I think it's in Mama's number book under D."

"Okay, okay Juno. I'll go." Keith hesitates, watching his mother.

Beth forces her eyes open. She sees her sons standing above her, looking down at her, two faces like two moons in the night sky. Her studio is darkened, the afternoon sun blended into evening and she is confused, wondering what happened. She was painting, the work turned out beautifully, and then what?

"Mama, what's wrong? What happened?" Juno asks, wringing his little brown hands over and over like salmons running the current.

"I mean, we came home, waited for you, called your name and you didn't come. And we found you here." Keith's voice sounded accusing.

"Are you sick?" Juno whimpers, his tears starting, his cheeks quivering, lips shaky and pink.

"Well, are you?" Keith asks, raising his voice.

Beth pulls herself up to a sit, ears ringing slightly, feeling drugged.

"I'm so sorry boys, I...I'm not sure what's happened. I was painting and I was probably in here too long. I, I just don't know."

"Mama, did you eat today?" Juno sits beside her, grabbing her hand, talking softly, eyes like water, the ripples on a morning lake.

"Prob'ly not," Keith answers, walking around her painting, round and round, looking at the trees.

"Did you eat, Mama?" Juno asks again.

"You know, honey, I think I forgot again. I had that salad you know...and then I had the coffee."

"That was yesterday after school," Juno whispers.

"Was it?" Beth searches her memory, trying to pull the two days together, tries to weave the night into morning into afternoon.

"Yes, it was."

"What is this, anyway?" Keith asks. "Since when do you draw trees?"

"I guess, today. I drew the trees this afternoon."

Juno stands, looking first at his mother sitting on the floor, then turning toward the oversized canvas and looking at the long branches, the outturned trunks, the breaking of earth where the roots pulse underneath. He leans in, eyes searching each stroke, taking in each swoop of pressure, application of colour, blend of feeling inside the picture.

"Wow," he whispers.

"What?" Keith asks.

"Neat, Mom."

"Since when do you find a couple of trees neat Juno?" Keith laughs. "You don't even climb them like I do. If anything, I'm the tree-man in the house."

"It's neat *and* scary."

"Scary?" Beth asks. "One thing I don't draw is scary pictures, honey. They are just a couple of trees, like Keith says."

"But why all the babies?" Juno asks, arms extended outward like an eagle, lost in drift.

"Babies?" Beth asks.

"What the heck? Babies?" Keith yells. "Juno, you're hollersinating! There's two big fat trees and the sky and the ground. That's it. That's all I see. *Babies?* Are you for real?"

"I didn't draw any babies honey. Tell me what you see, sweetie?"

"Yeah, *sweetie*," Keith taunts, "tell us what you see, sweet-pea, sweetheart, little plum bunny?"

"All the babies, sleeping, dead, or whatever."

"What?" The word hardly audible from Beth's indrawn breath.

"Dead freakin' babies?" Keith yells.

"Juno, show me what you see?" Beth asks softly, looking at her son, his brown cheeks shining, the evening's darkness playing on his face.

"Right here." His finger points at her picture, traces the ground under the trees. Beth follows his fingers, her heart beginning to pound, her mouth turning dry and little bead of perspiration starting to break out on her neck.

"Right here. All these babies. Just lying here, underground, their eyes closed. Some look like they're sleeping, but then I look again and they look dead."

His fingers trace a face coloured the same shade as the roots, the earth, blended in—and Beth begins to see. There are faces everywhere. Dozens of baby faces, bodies, perfectly formed, in various shapes, sizes, positions. Eyes all closed, some look peaceful, small smiles resting on their faces, some look restless, some have the look of discomfort, but all are sleeping, dead, some look protected underground, some look buried, some look discarded. Tiny fists balled together, fingers wound through each other, little toes perfectly formed. There are boys and girls blended together, piled on top of each other, bodies haphazard wrapped in roots, wound together by limbs and root and earth.

"My God," Beth whispers. "My God, you're right."

"Mama, why did you draw this?" Juno turns around and asks.

"I … I'm not sure." She doesn't know how to answer and cannot take her eyes off the artistry, the perfection of these small bodies. "I can't say that I know."

"You two aren't making any sense." Keith huffs. "I don't see any babies and I don't see the point of this conversation."

"I … I'm not sure I know why or remember why," Beth answers.

"Did you both hear me?" Keith speaks louder.

"Yes honey, we did." Beth turns to her fair son, his handsome face, his pink-tipped ears.

"Are you alright then?" Keith snaps. "I mean, we come home from school, you're gone, we freak out, we're hungry, no dad as usual, no supper, and here you are conked out from starvation and so we gotta go hungry, too. Next thing we'll be on the floor passed out from hunger."

"I'm so sorry, honey. I lost track of time and I forgot to eat and I guess it got the better of me. I'm sorry. It won't happen again. Go on down and I'll come down in a minute and whip up something for all of us."

"Fine. Do I have a choice?" Keith storms out of the room, the door slamming behind him.

"Geez, do I ever do anything right in his eyes?" Beth asks, feeling pale, sickly, old.

"He loves you, mama. I think he had a another fight today with Buck, that big kid in grade six."

"Oh no." Beth shakes her head. "I'll have Daddy talk to him tonight. He always knows the right thing to say to him. I always say the wrong thing."

"But I do like the picture, Mama." Juno admires the painting, flicking on the lamp on the end table. "It is the neatest thing you ever drew. I was just surprised, that's all. You never draw people, that's all. I didn't even think you could draw babies that good. They are real-looking. Real good."

"Thanks, Juno. I didn't think I could, either. I think we're both surprised. Come on, sweetie. You must be hungry, too. Let's all go down and have a bite to eat. Come on."

"Are you sure you're okay, mama? I was real scared, watching you all laid out on the floor like that." Juno's cheeks shake briefly.

"I'm okay, I promise. I'm just hungry and feeling weak from not eating. I can't keep forgetting to eat. It's not right."

They walk together to the door. Beth reaches over and flips off the lamp, ruffling her son's hair.

"But mama?" Juno asks, before he closes the door to her studio.

"Yes, baby?" she asks as they stand in the hallway.

"Where are all the mamas?"

"Mamas?"

"Yeah." He pauses. "You drew so many babies. But where are their mamas?"

Beth doesn't answer right away. She closes the door and leads Juno down the hallway toward the kitchen. "I don't know, my boy. That's the truth. I really don't."

11

Jolene

SHE LET HERSELF DRIFT ON THE DRUMBEAT, the voices of women. She floated in the darkness like water, like blood, like the heat of bodies enmeshed.

Mama's leg is warm against Jolene's cheek. She always falls asleep on her mama's leg while her mama scratches behind her ears. The wind howls. Stormy springs in Ontario are the worst; the wind can be heard every night, howling, screaming, chasing the animals into tree trunks, scaring all the people indoors at suppertime. Mama moves slightly, gently enough so that Jolene's head does not slide from the side of her thigh. Jolene is afraid tonight, worried that the rain will push through the walls, tear into her sleep, rip her from this life she knows. The walls of the house aren't strong, she knows that. She knows that her mama's brothers built the house and she doesn't think they really knew what they were doing. She remembers her mama muttering *This old shack will just fall onto our heads one night, the walls are just gonna topple on over.*

She clings to her mama, frantic, distant. Lighting flashes over the walls, the flowered couch, the bedspread with daisies over it, the old heater in the corner that glows red and has long spirals, hot and orange that look like rows of horrible smiles. Her mama's face flashes, the cigarette to her lips, sucking, sucking, the ash long and twisted. The lighting flashes again and her mama doesn't move, doesn't jump and Jolene thinks she is brave and strong. She looks at the trail of bruises down her mama's face, the thick ring of red around her throat and she hates this day forever.

Dreams want Jolene, but she won't give in to them. She wants to be with her mama today and she will make herself stay up all night just in case he comes back. She knows her mama is crying because she smells her tears, but she knows she will not make a sound. She never does.

Earlier, before the rains, she wades into the lake, looking for a dead fish. She knows the fish feel the storm before it comes.

But how, then, did you know it was coming?

She wants to catch the dying fish, fry its flesh for her mother, present it to her sizzled perfectly, its skin silvered, withered from the heat of the pan. She wants her mother's eyes on hers, needy, hungry. She wants her mother to lie back when she is finished eating, and sleep, and forget, and breathe the in and out of calm, a cusp of peace, an edge of forget. She craves a protection for her mother, even if it never comes. So when the first wave hits, knocking Jolene over, she can't stand, can't find her mother and her mother's boyfriend anywhere and the water fills her nose, and she can't see her mother, can't breathe anymore. Later, when her mother finds her, she carries her home, up the long hill, through the bush, the trail that wound to the back of their small house, her mother's boyfriend's voice keeping her alert.

You fucking idiot! What if she drowned? You'd lose her to the CAS and probably go to jail or worse. You're too busy strumming that damned guitar instead of watching your daughter. She always wanders, you know that. You need to quit slurping your wine, take a breath of fresh air instead of smoking your cigarettes and pay attention.

Her mother listens all the way back to the house. She puts Jolene down on the couch and then she turns to her boyfriend. The fight lasts for hours. Jolene drags her blanket under the table, feeling safer, feeling closed in and less afraid. She likes it under the table with the long smoke-stained tablecloth covering almost everything but their feet. Her mama with her long, brown toes and red chipped polish that they were supposed to redo. His with his Adidas running shoes, dirt-crusted and making the floors dirty, filled with mud from beside the lake. She sees the lamp smash beside the table, a small shard of light bulb landing near her knee. Jolene picks it up and looks at it, its shine, its jagged point, the perfect reflection of her eye on its surface. The eye blinks and Jolene looks closer, rubbing the edge of the broken glass with the side of her finger. Blood pops out of a slight scrape and it doesn't hurt, just feels heated and cool and the sounds grow louder, her mother's feet running around the table, a hand smashing on top of the table, limbs gnarled around and around each other, black hair on the floor, his hands, blood and dirt, his fingernails dirty, his mother's breaths, loud and panting and Jolene cuts into the side of her hand, and it doesn't hurt, not really, and the red is quite pretty like a ladybug or her mother's lipstick or the crest of a woodpecker, pounding and pounding and pounding away.

The storm begins in earnest, the thunder drowning the sounds of her mother's voice, the falling of bodies. Jolene is afraid and she tried to close her eyes, but sleep won't come, not tonight. Her hair is still wet from the water and her chest still hurts from the effort of holding her breath underwater. Her ears still ring and her stomach feels sore from holding in her tears. Jolene imagines herself still stuck in the water, standing knee-dip in the water, letting the storm tear into her and feed on her flesh, opening herself up to the clouds, the gnawing pinpricks over her skin, feeling destroyed and preserved all at once.

And then later, when the house sounds and body sounds stop, Jolene crawls out and looks at her mama sprawled on the long, sunken couch. Seeing the silence of her mama's pain, Jolene pulls her mama to her and weeps, her long hair covering them like a cloud, their combined flesh a cool laughter, a vicious joy unbroken. Only then can she sleep, her fingers counting the strum of her mama's wristbeats, counting them like they say to count sheep until the blackness folds over her like a casket, or a long pathway whose light is drowned by branches.

In the sweat Jolene smelled sage starting to burn, cutting through the weight of heat like a breeze. The first waft was the best, and the suddenness of it threw her off balance, brought fragments of mother-memory sharply into focus—her guitar, her stale cigarette smoke seeping out from under her door, her midnight promises, her perfume that Jolene still wears, one drop at a time, forgetting her face sometimes without it. She saw a fraction of her mama's face, heard the words her mama said when she was certain Jolene was sleeping. *I love you my girl. I'll be back for you soon.*

Her tears and the sage and the drumbeat and the women singing—all were braided together under the blanket of heat.

12

The Grandmothers

THE HOWL OF THE CROWNING was when one stood and whispered words of quiet to the woman. Wiped down the sweat, loved her more in her breathlessness, her desperate fear.

That minute. Crucial. Find a spot and watch it, focus, recede into a memory, a carving, become something other than this, for a moment. Find a rhythm. Like weaving. The rhythm is crucial, musical even, an even in and out, the fingers flying back and forth, brown fingers in the midst of creation. A basket forming, a new birth.

The howls that came from their own throats frightened them. The carnality, the spittle flying, the wide open splaying of the legs, the woman-lips stretched, tissue held together by tissue, the dark hair slipping in and out, unsure of which side is safer. Pink and black, the merge of colour, the red shock of blood, the clear saliva, a flash of forehead flesh, the purple howl of the new mother. The colour of love in the hands beneath the armpits of the woman. Lifting, coaxing, breathing strength in the ears, the sound of experience, the mother flesh a reassurance of the cycle. The howls that came from their own throats frightened them.

This one, she fainted when the baby's face emerged, face whitened by the movement, lips bloodied and dry, flesh seared by the transference of life, the little face thrust forward, silent, round and soft, waiting. Us women held her body, bathed her into wakefulness, her body limp, bronzed, naked and full, restless movements in her belly settling. The black tunneled away from her and her wail returned in force. Now she opened her eyes.

"Yes."

That was all she said and she pushed with the last of her strength.

"Here he comes," she whispered.

And the girl opened her eyes with the shriek, with her son's first wail of life.

The Grandmothers gathered together, catching the tiny body, clearing his breathway with browning rods, and placed him on his mother's breasts, full-veined, throbbing, prepared for release. Milk-tipped, glistening.

"Wait now," the girl said.

"Relax. Let the child suckle."

"It's not that."

The girl clutched her stomach, felt frantically, alive in her sweat, eyes wide, knowing.

"There is another," she whispered, eyes heavy, exhausted.

The Grandmothers gathered, wove around each other and felt her stomach, some hands smooth, some hands wrinkled and worn. The oldest Grandmother stepped forward.

"She is right. Let's continue."

They gathered in a tight circle. The baby gurgled, lips over flesh, finding his mark. The mother felt her milk release as she prepared to push again, not knowing if she could hold onto his slippery flesh. The baby pulled the liquid from her breast in long, thick gulps as she bore down in silence.

13

Beth

TWICE NOW CLOSE TO LOVE. TWICE, THE TWINGE, the falling under, the blend between the world and the unnamable thing that pounds the heart out of the body, the senses, the concrete push of thought. She wonders at this, alone, green tea steeped on the table, feet up, feeling guilty for her lack of duty. The kids are tucked in, sleeping. Her husband has fallen asleep on the bed fully clothed again. She didn't even realize he was home until she saw his black polished shoes out of the corner of her eye while checking on the boys upstairs. She left him, not wanting to wake him, craving some time alone desperately. She turned off the bedroom light that he left on, and tiptoed downstairs.

She sips her tea and remembers the first time she saw the boys. First time they were placed in her arms, one by one. One with fine, blond hairs over his head, so fine and light that the pink of his scalp showed through, the pulse of his soft spot on his head throbbed and throbbed. Vulnerable, she thought, so delicate. Breakable. She was frightened. Then the other one was placed in her arms. Black hair, long, thick, coarse. So different, she thought, so unlike each other. But the faces were exact. Their cries were identical. Their sidelong looks were synchronized. Their eyes closed in sleep at the same time, breathing calmed, lips jumping in dream. She leaned back, exhausted from watching the two of them, love descending on her like an eagle's landing, laying her flat, afraid for her future, clutching the two small bodies, drowning in her own sweat that prickled like talons through her backflesh, lifting her, lifting her higher than she wanted to be.

She pulls her robe tighter around her body, part in response to the memory, part reflex. She wonders about herself as mother. *Is she good enough?* So much guilt, so much pleasure. The filling of hours with her children to erase those blank times that she had as a child, those quiet times where no one came, where no one peeked around the corners to talk, to see how she was doing. Blankness as a page is beautiful. It is the breath before creation, the pull of thought, the inspiration before the luxury of fulfillment. But when you are waiting, it is ugly. It is a black thing in the corner, a curled deep ball rolling over itself, hungering for its own bones, gnawing deeply, the only way it knows how; a huge black pit in the earth, waiting for someone to walk over it. The wait is long and silent. A perfect graying, the simplicity of death easing into the long span of life. A breath, a cool morning, a tilt of the chin over a coffee cup, steamed into a formation of flesh; not white, not black. This is the wait of vacuity. But to own it is different. So much more, so much less than anything. A deepening crevice, continually shifting. The void expanse, widening, creaking with its movements. She pulls her robe tighter, shivering, feeling squished as a cocoon in all of this white wrapping.

Sweat

This house owns her in some way. She really wanted life here. Here more than anywhere. The first pull when she saw the long staircase, the familiarity of the oak banister, the rows of pine lining the yard. Familiarity? She grew up on the reserve, the only oak being a sole tree out near the swimming hole, or a miniature replica of a canoe that she would put acorns in, and push across the living room floor, the scent of dog fur and firesmoke in her nose, a waft of childhood, an iota of history indulging her as brief as a first kiss. Her home that she ran from so young, strong legs carrying her out, her mother's tears as she packed a torn bag of her sister's, not wanting to look back like Lot's wife did, like the story she remembered from the church. She didn't want to die a pillar of salt. That voice, its spinning—the catapulting the landing the sprawling, that raced behind her to bangishimog. She wanted to die flesh and blood and guts and courage and strength and scream after scream of sweaty living ache flying out of her and so she ran and ran and ran and didn't look back to see what might attach itself to her yearning. To see what might follow her out the long stretch of highway, beside the rez dogs, beside the milkweed ditches where she stretched out her childhood, her sisters beside her, the whole world so far, far away.

When Beth left home, her mother pressed a wad of bills into her hand. *Go Elizabeth. Don't come back until you get whatever it is that you want. I don't want you to go but I know you have to. Now go, before your father and sisters wake up. I love you baby girl. Now go and make me proud.* Her little sister on the doorframe, brown shoulder inching forward. She wanted to say goodbye but her words were swallowed by her father's glance. *But we said goodbye. Her eyes and mine, the sound of the sun on our backs, the slanted pillow that I left, the twisted hair, curled like burning. Those little hairs caught in the woodstove, which the sides of your hands would catch and discard*

71

in the underside of the burning. Our eyes meeting when my shoulder scraped the edges of her simple mouthing. Little scuffles beside the fire. Baby sister, her low eyes finding mine. She was peeking around the stained doorway, her stuffed monkey caught in the underskin of her arm, her pyjamas slanted. I knew she wanted me to stay. I knew her sleeping, those dreams and legs and soft breath, my cheek. We watched the moon cut our windowsill like butter. The hill of her cheek the last thing I remember. Zahgidiwin. The stain crooked, the half words, the moon its feast, my memory. Waking—that arching road, the scent of stain painting history. Walking, the sounds sinking.

She never saw her mother again. She died suddenly the following winter of a fast pneumonia, choked beside her father in the night and nobody heard her. Beth dreamed of this for years, knowing that if she had been there, she would have heard her and saved her. Knew that if she hadn't left home to run off to art school, that her mother would have lived. Beth's guilt ate at her and her mother's face was beside every canvas, every mother and daughter that she saw at restaurants, cinemas, poetry readings. When Beth came back for the funeral, her father did not look at her until she was ready to leave. Beth lifted herself from the side of her mother's small pine coffin, her face so waxy and so unlike her that Beth had to turn away, could not pray, could not say goodbye properly. Beth's sisters wept and begged her to call more, to send pictures, to write or something, anything. And then she heard his voice.

My girl, come here. Come on home. Old eyes so thick and runny and reddened bags so heavy.

And she ran to him, her ear against his chest almost knocking him down, and his hands were bony against her spine and he smelled of the air and firewood, and she knew he missed her and didn't hold her responsible for her mother's death. She couldn't look at him when she left but she knew he was watching his first daughter and blessing her life and that she would never see him again either.

She sips her strong tea, loving the burn in her throat, the heat in her belly, the long insistence that pushes into her, waking her, and making the guilt of the years slough off slightly like a fine scattering of seed at her feet, and it is not enough, but it is something.

14

Jolene

THE SWEAT PERSISTED. ELSA SANG LOUD AND STRONG, her voice a waking dream, her voice a chant that edged Jolene into a comfort and she heard her own voice join her, the words bursting forth, a tongue that she did not recognize. She was not self-conscious, was not worried that the other women would find her stupid or out of place, or would think that she should not sing these Ojibway songs with a tongue that did not know Ojibway. She felt the music, followed Elsa's lead and soon was lost in the sound of the drumbeat, singing along with the others, allowing herself to return to a past that she had safely put away in her heart, choking it out until it was ready to burst and explode and drip out from her mouth in large, bulbous pieces.

Jolene is placed in a foster home that winter. The authorities find her hidden behind the cold woodstove on a mattress covered with quilts, shivering. She thinks it is her mama returning. She sits up in her blankets, straining her attention, hope hurting her throat, making her sweat and cry before she sees the faces. She wants her mama back so bad, good or bad. Her mama is good, she knows that. The bad times were not so bad and Jolene understood why her mama made some of the choices she did. She didn't ever mean to hurt her, she didn't ever mean to leave her, Jolene knows that. Jolene knows that her mama is good, Jolene knows that she will come back, sooner or later. So when she hears the knock at the door, hears the door scraping open, when she hears the voices, she is sure her mama is there to get her, to take her to a new apartment, in a new city, to start over, and pretend that this never happened, or to at least explain that there was some emergency, some tragedy, some great thing that kept her away from her only baby, left in a house in the bush with no one at all, no one, no sound, nothing at all to hold onto.

Two women and a tall man with glasses already frosting up from the cold and a long woolen coat come in and they stop when they see her, not saying anything. The older woman moves first, her voice cracking to see the little brown face pushed out of the blankets, to see the skinny cheeks and the bony hands clutching at the quilt so tightly, still so strong, still so alive and so ready.

Jolene, right? I'm Mary Canyon and we are here to talk to you and to bring you someplace warm.

Where is my mama? Did you come with my mama?

We will find her and we will bring her to you once we find her. We are here to help you.

But did she send you?

No Jolene.

Why are you here?

We received a call. Someone saw you looking for wood in the bush. They were surprised to see you, thought you'd left with your mother.

Who called you? Why didn't they come in and find me then?

Jolene, we will explain it all to you. Please, let me help you up into our warm car. We will take you someplace warm, have a hot meal. Maybe a hot chocolate? Please come. We are not here to hurt you and yes, we will help you find your mother.

With the mention of her mama, Jolene breaks and cries for the first time that winter. Her shoulders shake and the quilts fall off her shoulders and the authorities try not to gasp at the sharp bones poking out of her shirt, and the largeness of her teeth and jaw from the lack of food, at the horrific appearance of this child. Jolene lets herself be lifted, lets them wrap her in the blankets and take her out of her mama's house and lay her in the back of the car where it is so warm her head pounds, where it is so warm it feels like Heaven. Jolene only remembers sleeping, her head bouncing slightly on the backseat, where her head rests on Mary's lap like it used to on her mama's, only Mary is softer, smells of violets and baby powder, and her hand rubs her head the wrong way. But Jolene sleeps anyway.

Weeks later, she is placed in a foster home for the first time. Her mama isn't found and no one explains much to her except that she is going to a farmhouse with a nice family who will watch over her until her mama comes back. Jolene is fed toast and scrambled eggs and they drive her to a small farmhouse outside of Barrie. The nice lady Mary drives, playing soft music and trying to say nice things, but Jolene doesn't hear anything, just watches the world pass by and thinks that the long snow-filled fields looks selfish, taking over the whole world, and feels angry for the first time that she remembers. She no longer hopes, just wishes that she could sleep without dreaming and that time would go by fast until she is old enough to die without explaining anything to anyone. She tries not to want her mama, tries not to pull up the image of her face laughing over a morning tea and cinnamon toast, and knows that she will find her herself one day and knows that there will be a good reason for all of this. She watches her reflection in the mirror, thinking how ugly she looks in the dark, skinny and mean looking, and looks away, back at the white pressed fields blanketing the whole earth and leaving no room for anything else.

Jolene is introduced to Mrs. Kozlov, a stout, sturdy woman wearing a faded flowered dress, very much like the bedspread that Jolene's mother used on her long bed. Mrs. Kozlov looks Jolene up and down for several seconds, and then grabs her hands.

"She's really skinny," Mrs. Kozlov tells Mary.

"Yes, well, she hadn't had much to eat when we found her, in fact, she..."

"Yes missus, yes, I see," Mrs. Kozlov interrupts. "But she is thin. Are you sure she's healthy?"

"Oh yes. She's had medical attention. She is healthy. She may need some rest, some good meals and a bit of quiet before she settles in properly."

"Sure, sure," Mrs. Kozlov says, eyeing Jolene down with suspicion, a direct disapproval that Jolene feels and that makes her look to the floor feeling nauseous.

"I sure am tired though," Jolene states.

"Sure, sure," Mrs. Kozlov repeats. "I'll show you to your room then, where you can sleep. Unless you want a bite first. I can make an exception this time and feed ya some before you settle."

"No. I'm really tired," Jolene says, yearning for a pillow, a bed where she does not have to see these people or look into anyone's eyes.

"Fine. I'll take you then. Goodbye Mary. We'll bes in touch." Mrs. Kozlov turns and beckons Jolene to follow her through the dark kitchen.

Jolene turns and looks back at Mary and sees the older woman looking concerned and unhappy.

"Jolene. Take care now," Mary says. "I will be in touch."

Jolene stops and says "And if you...you know...if she turns up..."

"Yes, dear, yes. I will come for you immediately. I promise." Mary turns, wiping at her face.

Jolene continues through the kitchen, following the flowered back with trepidation, into a dark hallway to a darker door at the end of a hall where the woman turns and says, "Okay, here ya goes. In ya goes to bed."

"Thanks umm...Mrs. Koz...Koz..." Jolene stutters, uncomfortable.

"Don't bother, it's a difficult name to some."

"Well, what can I call you then, ma'am?"

"Nothing. Yas don't need to call me nothing." Mrs. Kozlov turns and walks away, leaving Jolene to open the door and step inside.

Her room is a box. Desk with carved indents and initials battered into its flesh, black stains and wood-eyes glaring into her. There are little fuzzballs in the corners that wave back and forth from edge to edge, lonely. The window ledge holds dark sludge inside of it, old hair, pieces of bugparts and a blackened match that still smells of sulphur. Jolene smells it sometimes, loving the scent, reminded of lighting the woodstove at her old house, the low light before the blaze, the aftersmoke that stuck in her flesh for days. Jolene falls into the bed and sleeps without covering herself up, sleeps through the night and into the morning, only waking to a loud knocking at the door, a harsh banging and a voice yelling.

"Come. It's breakfast-time. Come now. Up and at 'em. Get on down for breakfast."

Jolene stands and straightens her shirt and opens the doorway, walking the long walk to the kitchen, down the hall that stays dark no matter what time it is.

Sweat

Mrs. Kozlov cooks hours before the kids wake. Lumpy oatmeal and toast that, when served, is hardened and dried, the butter inside mushed and indented. She always swallows it down, fast, the toast edges scraping her throat raw, wanting jam to dilute the taste, wanting more than water to wash it down. Mrs. Kozlov is hard, everything about her. Jawline square like a box, clenched, a steady rhythm made by her teeth that muscle her cheek in and out as she stares out the window at the man on her tractor, the husband that she is waiting to scream at, to mutter to under her breath, laugh at long and hard for the kids around the table to see. Jolene likes to watch her from the back, wonder about this woman's life and how she became like she did. What made her hands shake in fear, anger, wrath? What brought her to this Ontario farmland from her country? Jolene hears her speak of her country with a shake of her head, a hard fist in her gut, but does not know which country she means.

Her own children, almost grown, never speak to the foster kids. Their eyes trace their bodies openly, gawk at the girl's faces, loose hair, sleep-puffed eyes, but they will not speak. Or blink. Two large-boned boys, almost grown, but not quite. Their bodies are massive, hands huge like two mitts, skin broken and chapped, some spots crusted over with scabby protrusions. The older one has a face like a puffy fish, one near death, before the final haul of breath, eyes bulged forward, lips pushed out in a constant exhalation. The other has the look of a rabid dog, ready to bite, pounce, pour his disease into the next flesh that happens by. Jolene does not look back at them. Some instinct keeps her attention on Mrs. Kozlov for protection, on the other girls, the smaller ones who find her hands under the table and clutch them, dig their nails into her flesh.

Mrs. Kozlov will walk in without knocking, the door flying open as though she will catch her at something wicked.

"Whatcha doing Jolene?" she will ask, not blinking, the wringing hands, the restless fingers in her dress.

"Nothing Miz, just sitting here."

"Why just sitting here? Bored? I got lots for you to do! You see that man in the field. Stand up and look. Just look. Four hours a sleep he gets a night. I'm sleeping when he comes in and sleeping when he goes back on out."

"Oh." Jolene begins to pick at the black window sludge, watching the thick-bodied man on the tractor in the field, his back humped under his flannel checked shirt. She doesn't like him for his silence. His silences. His quiet breaths that can take over a room when the children are eating.

"Well. What do you say then about that?"

"Huh? About what?"

"Honestly girl, I wonder if you're all at home in there. Get out of this room and help with dinner. No sitting around like this. No more. No more. All the other kids move around doing stuff, picking stuff up, washing and drying, you know, doing stuff. Even the little ones. But you, you just sits here dreaming of this in that. Get up now. Come with me. I'll teach you how to work. I knows where you're from and I'll bet your momma never showed you how to work. I seen lots of kids like you before. Lots just like you sitting up in their rooms not knowing how to work."

Jolene follows her, watches Mrs. Kozlov's hands yanking at her flowered dresses, rubbing the colours off of the flowers, graying everything, turning everything to smog, a choking haze that sinks into skins quicker than a matchscent. She follows this woman whose scent falls over her down the wallpapered hallway for years, to the kitchen where she chops onions, the tears falling over the brown of her hands, the white on brown looking curiously like burnt skin, an image she will dream about one day, wondering where it came from.

Sweat

Jolene shuddered, feeling burnt by the heat of the sweat, returning gratefully to the sound of Elsa's voice, the low humming that wound into her like the slow weaving of a basket, an artistry that made her smile in the dark, happy to be back in the present.

15

The Grandmothers

ONE LAY DOWN BESIDE THE NEXT and the next and the next. A succession of brown-coloured women spread across miles of steel beds. The beds were hard and uncomfortable, without pillows or sheets. Steel blocks on legs spread across miles of hard-soiled concrete land. A grandmother felt her spine press into the steel of the bed and tried to shift to a more comfortable position. This only rubbed the cord of her spine further and so she stopped, breathed deep, and waited. She heard the breaths of the other grandmothers beside her. Some deep and controlled, others short pants bursting out of trembling lips. The younger women clutched the edges of the steel frames. The older ones lay calmly, expecting this, knowing of this from the colour of the winds that passed through their lands over the years. From the sound of the cities, the changing footwalks of their mothers steps. The new tastes of the mornings or the dying drumbeats of the elders. Expecting this and so they waited. When the younger ones began to sob, the others made clicking noises with their tongues or reached their hands out sideways to brush a finger, try to pat a hand. The steel was cold on their spines, long indents of pain through their bodies, the cords of their backs numbing.

The doctors' footsteps were even, in synch with each other, the thousand doctors that walked toward the grandmothers' bodies. Some grandmothers now realized for the first time that they were naked, wondered why they didn't realize it before or feel the cool air shouting over their bodies. Skins pressing upward, layers of living exposed, experiences marking their bodies, pain and joy and the hunger of their want. The younger ones tried to hide themselves, cover themselves in fear, in protection. The older ones lay back at ease, expecting this, their bodies an expression of their lives, a soul-covering, simple and wrinkled. Some slept, others began a soft chant under their breaths, while the younger ones began a deep gurgle of fear that pushed outwards from their lips, sounding like underwater expulsions, sounding like the wind pushing at a door, ready to burst it open.

The doctors pursed their lips. Some paused, thinking. Others were brisk, ready to perform the business at hand. The younger doctors carried clipboards to take notes and the older doctors chuckled at them, sharing an inside joke. A grandmother screamed out in her tongue, *Ajinjagaayonh! Ajinjagaayonh!* her old lips open like a bird in mid-shriek, her bronzed lips shrieking and sending a low and long echo through the endless room. The doctors looked at each other, unsure for the first time, but continued toward the women, intent, driven by something darker than the tongue of this woman, a simple old woman screaming words that they would never understand. This grandmother quieted and the women breathed in unison. United together in their breathing, the image

83

of a hand beating on the tight pull of a drumtop to lull the succession of brown-coloured women spread across miles of steel beds. The breaths of the younger women and girls quieted also, sensing a change in the air. Their fear became deeper and their breathing internalized until their chests hurt. The doctors pursed their lips observing the women.

Some of the women were beautiful, young. Long and brown and lean, full in their womanskin, taut bodies breathing softly, then quicker, quicker. Some of the women were shriveled, their legs thin and wrinkled, eyes sunken in a fearful wisdom that the doctors could not look into. Instead, they first loomed over the young women, who began to cry. This was the easiest way to begin.

"Don't worry," a young doctor told a young woman, "It will be over soon." He lifted his hand as though to rub over her hair, and then changed his mind.

The knives glinted over the bodies of the women, severing pieces of their bodies with calm, swift movements. The women were silenced, their agony reverberated into their spirits and they were silenced, spliced into quiet, a darkened sound, outside of peace, into an abyss forced to open, an intruded cave where nobody belonged. The grandmothers watched as the wombs of the young women ascended into air, floated above the heads of the doctors, and were extinguished forever. Fallopian tubes created pathways outside of motherhood, a vacant loneliness, a craving that these women would taste somewhere deep for centuries to come. The ovaries of the women cried together, tried to bury themselves deeper into the women's bodies, a sound like raindrops onto leaf, a dying ebb.

The doctors dug deeper, their arms quick, frantic. The doctors dug into the bodies of the women, their eyes intent, their hands quick, sweat beginning on their brows. The womanblood stained the doctors' flesh, sank in deeply, untraceable, unwashable. The doctors pulled back, finished. They nodded at each other as they made off through the door, the women staring empty at the ceilings that were skyscapes where their unborn children waded with each other in bloody rivers, stolen from their mothers, taken by stiff, white hands that flung them silent into this place of dreamlessness, searching.

The grandmothers formed a circle around the young women, around their beings, and could smell their scents and desires. The older women knew that these young women would never be mothers, knew they would desperately hold their sisters' babies and cry for their own. A grandmother looked behind her to see a doctor calmly sipping tea, his bloody fingers casually stroking the side of a cup, leaving thick traces of the massacre on the side of the china. He smiled at a picture of his family on his desk, his teeth long and straight like rows and rows of gravestones.

16

Beth

HIS LEG COOL, HER HAND SWEPT OVER IT. Hairs risen, she continued. His sleep destroyed, she climbed over him, covered him fully, raising her body over his, hair falling, breaths parting like the edge of sea and shore. He didn't wake, he no longer slept. Somehow, his thrusts met hers, pushed her up, peaked into her as a wave would meet the sky. He edged inside her. His hardness filled her open body, made her whimper, and think of newborn puppies, the separation of liquid and air. He pushed her in and out of dream. She swallowed sweat and flesh, choking. She was lifted by a thick cord of sinew, a cattail that did not end, that reached past histories. In this blackness, she tasted seaweed, was pulled along an underwater corridor, pushed forward, a long redness pulsating tightly around her, a salty waterbeat edging along her flesh. The sweat of birth, a womb of creation, the making of pinkened aching, the arching, the arching, crying, singing. Her voice rose. She continued strumming his body, inching into his emerging, until the cry escaped, pushed her outside of herself, black hair flung low on her back, his hands, his hands welting her, his hands molding her like a precise potter, practiced, perfected, polished.

Panting, she slept, his hands heavy on her open thighs, sweat down her belly like tears, shameful and joyous, but free, free. Sleep came too easily, and she knew she should be suspicious. His body fell too simply beside hers, and she thought that she should have gotten up and made the lunches for the kids for the next day. Her hair held her head like a thick pelt, warm and soft. She thought she heard the nightsounds of the bush. She thought she was back home in childhood. She thought she might be awakening.

Somehow she dreams. The same one again, nothing new or different, maybe the background a shade or two lighter, or the air scent a bit thicker, but the same thing again. She is falling, unafraid. It is not a frightening thing, this dream. Its colours are luminous, bright. Pinks and crimson glowing through white sheers and crimsons alive behind the walls of tissue that billow like curtains in the low spring, like grass inside of a new breeze, this billow as a pulse, and she swallows and it tastes like morning again and morning again each time, its newness stirring life in her again and again. She is falling, unafraid. The air feels like it is corded, as though she is being held by the hands of the dead, but this is not frightening, either. The dead here are just making their presence felt. They are not here for anything else, just to hold her as she falls, just to place their spirit hands under her flesh, caress her through this space. Her flesh swallows their spirit-breaths as she falls, sucks them in and saves them up, each pore overfilled; she receives their offerings, each of their gifts as she falls.

Here, one says, taste my joy, this is birth—not the release, but the conception. Taste the joy of two loves coming together in creation. Taste the solidity that emerges from this, two bodies coming together as quick and as painless as water, merging as one, and the tears inside of joy, oh the tears of love are sweeter than those of pain. Taste this and love until your last breath.

Here, says another, take my pain and use if for strength. We are women who eat this pain and grow larger for it. This won't shrink you or hurt you, but enlarge your vision. Just take it, swallow its sourness, chase it with the cleansing from that raincloud, but take it, dear one, and let me live with you and teach with you and make you recognize others who need, others who have eyes like mine.

While falling, she feels comforted by the hands of the women-spirits, feels welcomed and loved, feels like she is in the middle of a great feast of offering and she accepts their hands, their love, the voices and guidance found inside the depths of the wind, the free air, the long drift downward. She knows that she has never felt this kind of kinship before, this freedom of receiving without giving and there is no guilt at all. No guilt, no shame in the taking. She loves these women-spirits and wants more of them, more of their words, their hand-warmth on her being, and she knows she is safe here, this place of breath and windspace.

And she is falling, unafraid, her clothing falling off her body like smoke. Her nakedness feeds off the air, collecting scents that have been lingering for centuries, falling inside others' years of dreaming, her breasts lifting under her chin with the airflow, her flesh gathering the learning in the spirit-laughter as she is falling. She feels a hum gather inside her legs, a womansong of water. Her lips open, multifolding the air. The flowing begins to sing, a pinkness exploding as she prepares to connect with the earth, a liquid drips down her thigh, a heat in the center of her body opens, burns out of her into the air, making a huskier scent, one as old as the sky; a beat of blood makes her cry out and it is beautiful, such a ringing of love, it is beautiful this womanhood escaping and she feels the water between her thighs and the drip of love, a laughter all around her and the grass is cool on her skin, her landing is a slow dive underwater and she lies there on the grassbed her pinkness being strummed by history, by the breath of all creation, by a hand as large as thought itself.

She awoke, desperate to return.

17

Jolene

THE SWEAT WRAPPED AROUND HER. She was more comfortable now with the heat, the memories, the sensations of history entwining itself to her present, marking her soul. Her shakiness had stopped and the feeling of being an outcast was fading. She was starting to feel as though the darkness was safe, a security enveloping her, keeping her from harm. Strangely comforted, she felt her body relaxing and accepting the solitude, the deepness like the middle of a dream, or like a thrust of the underwater that a swimmer must feel.

Jolene feels called by the past, by voices invading her, twisting her toward them. And again, and always, her mother. A voice like stucco, prickly, soft when broken, turning into chalk onto the fingers. Mothers. Mothers who disappear, their trails ending abruptly, their names nowhere to be found no matter which city you step into. Their scents that follow you through life, taunting you. Can smells be so cruel as to whisper out of other women's necks and wrists, laughing, laughing, a high pitched cackle that chases itself into your dreams?

Jolene has a habit. She collects phonebooks from every city she enters. The nights hitchhiking, the rides from strangers, from truckers and men who demand payment from her shivering body after a long rain, her shirt soaked, hair stringing into her eyes, looking for a place to sleep, a quiet place where she feels safe. The cities, the lights, the farmlands, the travelling, the search for a home that never manifests, a home that is lost to a dark bush with protective arms around it, barricading her out.

Some nights, drunk, bored, at a house party, she will search phonebooks, looking for her mother's name, a clue. Her mother has vanished, has gone missing one night, never seen or heard from again. How does that happen? How does a woman say goodbye and never be heard from again? She reads headlines, buying newspapers from each city, reserve, village that she passes through. She dreams of finding her mother this way. *Another Native woman slaughtered, no trace of any living relation.* She dreams of stepping forward to claim her mother's life, to identify the body. To acknowledge the long black hair caked with blood and smell the perfume still left on her corpse, nodding, *Yes, this is her. This is my mama.* Sometimes this would be easier. She piles these phonebooks in a box in her Auntie's shed, wraps them in garbage bags so the rain doesn't wilt them, so the snows don't destroy them. She keeps them just in case she misses a clue and can return to them. Names in garbage bags, piled and piled, wrapped together, her hidden secret.

Elsa's voice rose beside her. Drumming cooled her body, heated her mind. The sweat was in full fire. She felt the beat of the woman's hand beside her fall onto her drum. Flesh on flesh. She inhaled buckskin, licked her lips to taste salt and smoke. Fell into the music around her, leaning against the softness of the hides behind her. She was okay here. She was free to continue her living dream.

Faces swim around her. Babies she doesn't recognize, mothers that she somehow distrusts but wants, grandmothers that frighten her with their attempts to embrace, men reaching out to her, their tongues whispering things that she pretends to understand. She leans back, is told that their bodies would be closed off from their children, all who will die with the taste of their spiritbabies in their memory, a sense of loss so deep that they grow old quickly, ashamed of their motherlessness, staring at the water, searching. Hearing the future collecting itself briskly. Searching.

Here, she wonders if life is like a dream? Do you suddenly wake up and laugh at what you've been dreaming about? Does everything suddenly fall into place upon waking and you are flooded at relief that it was just a dream? It feels like a dream, this observing each feature at length, trusting no one, offering words to none. Some are beautiful, black hair flowing, lips laughing, eyes settled with peace. She watches as faces swim around her, each one presenting itself, and then falling away as simply as birchbark from a tree, floating up the riveredge in a rapid current.

One catches her eye. The face materializes into form, a neck, shoulders, long arms, torso, hips, legs, feet. Graceful, watchful, intense. Sits alone on a hilltop, waiting, looking downward, holding something small in brown hands.

She knows the person is aware of her watching, but neither of them makes a move to connect. She is enthralled by the movements of those hands. Small, quick fingerslices, weaving, flitting back and forth. There is something familiar there, but she is unsure what it could be. She has never seen anyone carve wood before. Little woodchips falling, make her feel like crying. She watches, drifts inside of the unseen creation slowly, until the carver speaks, not looking up.

"The tree I took this wood from cannot be trusted."

"Huh?" Jolene looks around, knows that the voice is speaking to her.

"Yeh. He tricked me, that tree." The carver's head shakes, smiles wryly. Jolene can't read it as old or young. The body appears young, and at this point female; the voice is male, and old as the sky.

"The tree tricked you?"

"Yeh." A laugh, which stops abruptly. Looks up. "Ever been tricked by a tree before?"

"No. Well, not really. Maybe."

"Not a good feeling, is it? Us people should be smarter than trees, don't you think?"

Jolene shrugs, "I guess so."

"That tree made my partner disappear."

"Your wife?"

"Well...yeh. Sure. Why not?" The hands stop moving. A long, thin piece of wood falls to the carver's knees. The face looks down, turns back to Jolene. Neither young nor old, and sometimes resembling a woman, is a woman, a boychild, a grandmother. Jolene feels cold. The longing in that face is familiar, mirror-like. "Beautiful, my partner. Like no other in this world. Or that world, for that matter."

"I...I'm sorry," Jolene sputters.

"Well, nothing to be done now. Nothing to be done now."

"If the tree is so clever, then how did you get the wood?" Jolene asks.

"Well, I saw him sleeping down by that embankment there." Chin nudges toward a steep hill overlooking a grassy field. "Don't look so surprised. Trees sleep too."

"I didn't know that."

"They do a lot of things you probably don't know about. Boy oh boy…" The sad face laughs and laughs, crinkling skin creating small lines around the eyes. The sun blasts hot in the laugh and she shivers in the heat.

"Well, how did you get the wood?"

"Oh, right. I chopped it off while he was sleeping. Just walked up to his sleeping bulk and chopped a limb off and ran. How's that for sneaky?" A deep, male guffaw, atop shaking female shoulders, looking young and old and so far, far away.

"What are you making?" Jolene bends in, trying to see.

"Well, I'm not done yet."

"Oh, I know, but I just want to know what it is. I can't see it from here." Jolene pushes herself forward, tries to see, tries to make out the dark shape in his hands. She can smell it, musky, alive, can feel it pulsating. She is drawn, mesmerized by the power of the wood.

"Like I said, I'm not done. Never let anyone see my carving till it's done." That smile again and Jolene feels life, feels like she is running, tastes grass under her feet, hears the current's force at the bottom of rivers—powerful, rich and pungent, the core of a seed, raw on her tongue.

"Aw… please."

"Wait Jolene, just wait."

"Hey, how did you know my name?" Jolene looks at the carver, curious.

"Hey, how do you know me?"

"But I don't, I don't. This is the first time I ever talked to you or saw you, or…" Jolene stops, breathless, as that face is replaced by the taste of her tears, as sudden and abrupt as a punch. They taste hard, seedy, they make her tongue hurt, the painful rub against delicate buds. They enter her throat and she hears herself moan.

Sweat

She feels longing. For a man. Not the kind of longing she is familiar with. Not for a touch to spread her open in the back of her car, in a hidden spot behind a house party or after the bar with him, his hands owning her, molding her. But a new longing. In a new place.

Jolene is suddenly aware of her heart. She feels a beating, fast and sure, living and beating and she is aware of her life. Why was she made? Why? Why? She puts her hands on her chest and holds them there, one on top of the other. The beats radiate throughout the flesh and bone of her hands. She remembers dreaming of cutting out her heart and holding it and examining it and cutting it open. And it was empty inside—no blood, no blood. Nowhere for the blood to travel, no passageways, no chambers, nothing. She remembers handling the sodden valve of her heart, finding it cold and unresponsive. She remembers the fear. Hard in her throat—remembers trying to suck in a breath. The pain in her chest. Remembers her dream, trying to stuff the dead heart back into her chest—better than nothing, right? Right? Isn't it? Her scream woke her auntie, who came running out toward her, the back of her slippers making a tap, tap, tap against the floor.

"Auntie!" she screamed. "Auntie!"

"What Jolene? For God's sake, what?" Her auntie looked down at her on the couch in fear.

"She took my real heart with her when she left." Jolene couldn't talk through her tears. "She took it with her."

Auntie looked around the room. "Who Jolene? Have you been drinking again?"

Jolene sat up on the couch. "Mama took my heart. I can't breathe without it. I can't breathe right. It is empty inside. Dry against my fingers. Like scraping a bone that's dried up in the sun, left on a long rock like those rocks up in Agawa."

Her Auntie felt her forehead and pushed her gently against the couch. "Jolene, you're burning up. You have a fever. Lie down and I'll get you a Tylenol. Lie down and relax. You're burning up."

She knew it was no fever. She knew she was dead, but how she kept walking and breathing and thinking she could not figure out. She knew she was dead.

But now, here in the Sweat, she can feel the beating. Can hear it like a drum in her ears. She is suddenly aware of the blood running in her veins and she remembers the bush as a child, how the rocks and dirt felt under her bare feet. Remembers the back of her mother's long skirt and how it felt pressed against her face when she hugged her legs. Perfume and cigarettes. She can feel her heart, knows that there is blood filling it up, can feel a warming in her wrists, under the long white scars. Scared that the blood will rip the scars open from the inside. Scared that her flesh will burst open from the inside and her new blood will pour out like a geyser and she will be down on her hands and knees scraping it from the floor, from the dirt of the Sweat and stuffing it back in her mouth, down her throat, swallowing, swallowing. She is hungry for this. Hungry for this.

Longing under the pounding. The new blood increases the longing and the tears soften on her tongue, the seeds sprout, take bud and enlarge slightly. A taste like yarrow emerges. Summertime yarrow on her back, the tickle of the leaf against her cheek, watching the world take place around her. Jolene remembers lying against the earth near her childhood home on the reserve, her mother searching for her. *Jolene! Jolene!* The thrill of hiding on her mother, a satisfaction found from her mother's worry. She was loved by her mother. Her mother was scared. Fear in her voice. *Jolene! Jolene!* Her mother wanted her. Wanted to find her. Six years old and lying low in the field behind her house. A glimpse of the waterline behind the pines. Six years old and sensing the thick of the yarrow under her cheek. Bending her neck and turning to the yarrow, the heat of the stem on her lips. Sucking the yarrow while her mother screamed and screamed for her. Swallowing the yarrow while her mother wanted her. Wanted her. Yarrow inside of her. Yarrow pulsing while her mother's hands found her. Lifted her. Carried her home with a bellyful of leaf and stem to warm her and heal her, resting her head on her mother's shoulder. She tasted it still on her tongue and she loved this day and loved this day forever.

Longing still under the pounding. *How do you know me? How do you know me?* The face and body are still there, smiling and whittling and chiseling the wood. The wood shifts form, becomes malleable, and the hands holding it form supple around the wood and she sees them holding gently a cornhusk doll, female hands cradling the doll. Jolene leans forward trying to find the face. The hands turn the cornhusk doll round and round and round, the body pliable in those hands, the body of the doll so still, arms flat and unmoving. An act of weaving, rows of twining fingers, so agile, so rhythmic. She wants to find the face. She needs to recognize herself in the face of the doll. She needs to find rest in the eyes, strain herself against the memory of weeping that might be found there. The tears are softer, no longer seedy in her mouth. Liquid tears as she examines the carver's face. She doesn't know how, but she knows him. Now distinctly a him. She remembers him. Longing still under the pounding. She leans against the structure of the Sweat. Remembers hands. Hands. Hands. Big hands. Always bigger than hers. Hands outnumbering each other, a quick succession of hands. Men's hands. Always bigger than hers.

Come with me, little girl. At her mother's party. Nine years old and he was leading her into her forest behind her house. *I want to show you something.* He looked like a nice man. Soft smile. Brown eyes, little hairs down the front of his hands. They were tiny blond hairs that looked soft and golden in the sun. At her mother's party. Her mother went into the house with her Auntie, her mother's lips were red with wine. It was afternoon and the sun was hot. Her mother wore a white dress with a long stripe of violet slashed through it. Her mother's lips were stained with red and Jolene thought it looked pretty. He looked like a nice man and he had little wrinkles at the corners of his eyes. She went with him. He showed her poison ivy, told her how frogs were so smart that after they hopped in poison ivy they would jump next to the plant that would cure poison ivy and rub themselves in it. Jolene laughed. His hands on her hands. Little wrinkles at the corners of his eyes.

She remembers her back against the tree. How her back scraped against the tree, how her back scraped hard against the tree, how the bark cut into her back when he lifted her. Pressed her against the tree. *Ouch.* He did not speak, just smiled at her with his eyes. Brown eyes, but not as dark as the tree. Little bits of oranges in his eyes. Little dots of oranges in his eyes. She could see herself in his eyes. Long brown hair, wisping out from the heat. Straight and wispy. Flyaway, her mother called it. She could see herself in his eyes. His hands lifted her skirt up and tore her underwear off. *Don't.* He did not speak, just smiled at her with his eyes. He looked like a nice man and he had little wrinkles at the corners of his eyes. She went with him. *Please don't.*

He did not speak. His hands were hurting her, trying to put something in her. She could see herself in his eyes and her own eyes looked round and did not blink. She could see little dots of oranges inside his brown eyes. Her back scraped against the tree. *My mother's calling me.* He was getting angry. He was trying to put something between her legs. He was getting angry. It couldn't fit and it was hurting her. He was grunting and he was getting angry. She squirmed. *Please don't.* She began to fall and her back scraped against the tree. It began to burn between her legs and she squirmed away from him. She fell. She saw him standing there. He was getting angry. His pants were down. How did that happen? When did that happen? His thing was poking up and he was rubbing it staring at her. She ran. He still watched her and rubbed himself. She ran back to the house, her heart pounding. She looked back and still saw his shadow in the bush. Her back hurt where it scraped against the tree. She found her mother in the kitchen drinking a cup of wine. *There you are my girl. Come here.* She crawled on her mother's lap and held on to her, watching the people that filled her house with a blank face, no one seeing her back, her heart pounding. Pounding. Pounding.

Jolene adjusts herself against the wall of the Sweat. Remembering hands. A man's hands. Against her throat. She met him at a party. In his car after the party, he put his hands around her neck, squeezed. She had tried to kiss him and he put his hands on her throat. She did not want to kiss him anymore. She could not scream anymore. Throat closing and her heart pounding. His fingers around her throat and he just watched her. Watched her choke. He had wrinkles around his eyes too. Green eyes, and then he let her go. Watched her stagger out of his car. Arms flat and unmoving. He laughed. *Stupid drunk Indian bitch.* He laughed.

More hands. On her breasts, squeezing. Between her legs. After parties. Men after parties. She thought she loved some of them. Thought some of them loved her back. Kissing these men, waiting for their hands on her. Letting them all have her, letting all of the hands own her. Hands balled up against her cheek. Her nose shattered once. The taste of blood and the pounding of her heart. She thought she loved that one. Lifted her hips against his: *iloveyouiloveyouiloveyou.* His baby in her belly, wanting to let him love the baby with her. *Get out of here, get rid of it. Don't come back till you get rid of it.* She didn't come back. Hid at her Auntie's, growing bigger and bigger.

Her mama's hands when she was small, her mama's hands with their polish, the smell of red, the painting, the red smile as she pulled Jolene's hands close to hers and painted her fingernails until they matched. Her mama was so beautiful and her hands were the most beautiful thing, wrapped around the side of a guitar, twanging the note so soft that Jolene's ear had to catch it quickly before it disappeared. Fluid, pliable hands that transformed sound and love into something gentle when she let them. The music in those hands, the perfect notes, the music that lulled her mind to sleep so slowly, not stopping until her baby was sleeping, the cigarette smoke a halo against her black hair, the silk that fell like a blanket, a field, a span as far as the universe can dream.

Hands creating her. Hands leaving her. Longing still beneath the pounding. She opens her eyes in The Sweat. The man is still watching her. He puts down the doll, wood splinters like rain blurring the edges of the doll's facelessness. *Come here my girl.* He extends his hands as though to hug her. She smells trees everywhere. Cedar. Oak. The memory of pine against her cheek. Maple branches waving. The dry crunch of leaves under her barefeet. He puts down his wood. *Come here my girl.* His hands. They are brown and have long lines down the palm. She closes her eyes and throws up everywhere, her legs hot with her own vomit. She begins to cry.

18

The Grandmothers

THE BABIES WERE THRIVING AND THE GIRL LAY DYING. Fat and sweaty, the boys lay on the skins, sleeping, bellies lifting and falling, their hands laid against each other gently. *Beautiful,* the women agreed. Twins. *Neezhoday.* The women gathered the babies to their chests during the day, nursing them with their own milk, sharing the milk from their own babies suckling with the twins. They ate heartily. The women wiped their chins with their fingers or a swatch of fur as they drank, admiring their vitality, their strength.

The first boy was fair. He was round and heavy, born big with rolls covering the small of his wrists. The women wiped the birth fluids from his crevices gently with sage water. *Mushkodaywushk.* Wiped his body with long fingers, cleansed him with the waters until his skin shone, glinted with a pinkened hue until he gurgled loudly and slept, tired from the long process, the many hands that loved him and touched him, the woman-fingers that he watched brightly with his blue-specked eyes until he slept. *Oningeen.*

The second boy, the dark boy, was thin, skinny with dark eyes that roamed the walls of the wigwam, traced the taut skin of the walls and the whittled poles and was silent. He watched everything and quietly observed each hand of each woman, barely blinking. The women rubbed him with the oils made of moosefat and his skin darkened and glistened, replenished the bronze and made his scalp shine. He did not smile, he did not move. The women worried slightly about his silence, his depth of quiet, but they had seen this before in watching an eagle before flight, a long journey that required a building of wills, and they accepted this child's ways and rubbed him, circulated his blood, and he too slept the sleep of those who have travelled long without stopping and who are finally permitted to rest.

The girl lay on a bed of furs inside of the wigwam, her black hair sprawled. The hair that once lay against her back like the glint of the side of arrowstone now lay flat and oily and pungent. Her mother bathed her hourly with herbs, praying over the sumac and burdock before applying it to her. The women waved sage over her body with cedar branches, pushed it toward her nose to inhale, wanting her to breath it in, absorb it into her tired body. They stopped the blood with thick, cleansed moss, but it kept coming, pouring out of her, so thick, staining her thighs with its fury. They expelled the milk from her engorged breasts and soothed her body with raspberry leaves, spoon-feeding her the juices from the edge of a leaf. Yarrow and red clover permeated the air. The juices ran out of her mouth and they wiped her chin with their fingers. They lay medicines on her tongue, hoping they would enter her body and begin to heal it. The girl breathed slowly, her belly rising up and down, the lines from the twins vertical slashes that the women salved with nettle, massaging her body tirelessly.

Sweat

The mother prayed, asked the Creator to heal her daughter who was barely a woman, asked the Creator to reach down and heal her for the sake of her babies, to take the sickness and to allow the medicines to work on her body. The women smudged, they prayed, the men lit a fire outside and they listened to the crackle from within the wigwam. The men sang and their footsteps comforted the women inside. The girl sighed and turned her head. The women watched her and continued their work, the tea-water brewing constantly, their cheekbones wet with juniper, braids damp with sweat and steam. Some held her hands, others sang to her quietly, some stood back and comforted her mother when she could no longer stand.

During the night, the women covered the girl with thick pelts and blankets while she slept. She cried out, whimpered and fell still. Each time she cried out, her mother, who slept beside her, cradled her head and whispered to her, *Gi zah gin, Gi zah gin*. When she heard her mother's voice, the girl settled and slept some more. The women changed the moss and dripped tea onto her tongue and lips. The mother whispered to the girl and with the mother's voice, the girl settled and slept some more.

Outside, a crack of thunder made everyone inside pause and the light outlined the shape of their bodies, stilled, until the first boy cried and they ran to his side, a dozen mothers surrounding the upturned face.

19

Beth

THE LABOUR WAS LONG, STARTING EARLY the morning before and running the full day through, the full night through and all through to the present day. She was too numb to scream, lost somewhere inside of a world of grey, of trickles of reality, little pieces of conversations, voices, snippets of life. This place was the ground on the edge of life. A world so far above the world she knew that she was surprised that she had never seen it before. There was a straight line that fell down vertically and so far that no bottom was seen. She knew that no one else could see it because between pains, she watched the doctors, watched the nurses, her mother, her husband, the passerby in the hallway, and they all smiled, looked worried, discussed casual things that let her realize that she was the only one here in this place of breathlessness, still breathing, still panting, ears still ringing.

Sweat

Beth's pregnancy went well. She looked beautiful from the beginning. All of the other things that other women complained about were easy for her. She never felt anything close to morning sickness, had no serious fatigue, backache or any crazy cravings. Her husband worked a lot, but he left little notes in the morning for her to see when she woke up. *Will try not to be late. You looked beautiful while you slept. Try to take a nap this afternoon. I love you. xo.* She felt amazing with her stretch of belly over her hips, once so thin and bony and now she felt full, alive, ready for a new beginning.

She painted a lot during her pregnancy. Fields of blowing cattails, birds flitting out of trees, a wide moon and crane balancing over the universe. She breathed her language to the baby. *Neegoosis. Neegoosis.* She knew he was a boy and she knew she'd name him Daniel, after her father. His grandpa. *Mishomis.* Her father always wanted a son. Beth's mother gave him seven girls, all beautiful, all talented, all so smart that her mother would tape their report cards to the fridge side by side and leave them there until the following year until they brought the new ones home, the old ones curling at the edges. *See Edith,* she'd tell her sister, *They just get smarter and smarter. I think they'll all go to university, like cousin Rita's boy. I think so. Maybe I'll have a doctor on my hands or even a teacher or a dentist. Who knows, right? My mother was happy I made it past the seventh grade. They will leave one day and I will let them. Go and take the world, I'll tell them.* And the laughter. Her mother with the long apron filled with little hummingbirds, tiny toes poking out of fuzzy blue slippers. She missed her mama's laugh, her father's long sighs as he watched the evening news on their small TV beside the kitchen sink.

Beth would bathe every evening, not too hot as to bother the baby in her womb, just warm enough so she felt sleepy, warm enough so that the baby was lulled to sleep by the placid pressure of the water, the slight splashing against the tightness of her belly, her long fingers massaging the bulge of her son slowly. Beth's body was long, legs still lean, browned by the summer, muscled from long years of stretching, running, lifting. Her belly shifted whenever the baby moved and she smiled, thrilled at the life inside of her, happy for a strong body to carry this baby from one world to the next. *Miigwetch,* she would whisper to the Creator of all things, *Miigwetch.*

The months passed smoothly. Her husband work steadily. *College fund, honey. We need to start saving up now. I need to work harder, harder, harder than ever. Don't expect me home until dark again.* She liked being alone. She really didn't mind her husband's long hours, the nights alone, the quiet times to reflect, to paint, to dip her body in her baths and dream of her baby, her new life, the gift that has been granted to her and her alone. The solitary days and nights and hours and minutes were spent talking to the life in her womb, painting round circles, round and round, buds blooming, moons to signify the shifts of time. Her hands were quick, fast, fingers flying through the hours, stopping only to eat, to nourish the life within her.

Sometimes she heard her husband come home after midnights. Sometimes she cracked her eyes open just a slice to watch him undress, take his tie off quickly, checking it for stains and then hanging it on his electric and revolving tie rack, the varying colours of his ties making prisms of colours like a palette, beautiful inside the glow of the moon through the window, so interesting beside his tired face, the smell of cognac that drifted with him into rooms like a worn perfume. She watched him undress, admiring his back and the taut muscle that hid under his thin dress shirts for no one in the world to notice. His back was long and low and dipped into his pants like a ski hill, a slope of hill falling, falling away inside of the black abyss of his trousers. He slid into his blue checkered pyjamas quickly as though he sensed that he was being watched, so fast that it was incredible, the stealth of it all. He sighed and never looked her way, just entered the bathroom, turned on the water and showered until he was raw, scrubbing himself waxen, every night the same ritual.

Beth closed her eyes and tried to fall back to sleep, the kicking of her son incessant, a mini woodpecker against her ribs. She turned and waited for her husband to come back out and to slide in beside her, nestle into her back with his chest, his slow heartbeat, always calm, never excited or afraid, his scrubbed nails, perfect and straight like his teeth, lines like a perfectly installed fence. Her beautiful husband whom she had been missing since she'd met him. The shower ended and the steam seeped out from under the door that he always locked and his footsteps echoed on the tile. He came out, closed the door, checked the windows to make sure they were locked, and slid in beside her. He did not nestle into her, their bodies did not touch. Beth wanted to turn around, but did not have the energy to make small-talk in the dark, didn't have the desire at eight months pregnant to try to make love or caress his shoulders. She closed her eyes and soon her breaths matched his, slow and steady, melting into one flat sound that got lost inside midnight, disappeared into the world and didn't bounce back.

She knew the minute that labour came. It came slow and so expected. Not the things that she read about, a bursting of waters, an expulsion of sound, a scream or a collapse. The world stood still and she just knew. The same as if she was going to blink again or take another breath. The same knowing that morning will come tomorrow and the earth will keep turning. She smiled and looked to the corner where her hospital bag was neatly packed, the baby's first clothes folded neatly inside, a warm little hat to cover his new head from the cool October air. Her husband was working. She would drive herself to the hospital, call him when she got there and then he would come. And then she would get to finally hold her son, love him to his face and let the world bloom around them both.

The nurse was kind and led her to the labour room, took her doctor's name and let him know that Beth was in labour. There was another woman sharing her room, but that was okay as Beth knew that the hospital in Sault Ste. Marie was notoriously understaffed and that there were never enough rooms for all of the patients. The room was blue and smelled of birds. She remembered finding a hummingbird dead behind her house and it was so tiny and she had never seen one up close and it reminded her of the scattering of hummingbirds painted on her mother's apron. Wings so still, wrapped in the grass, body tight and stiff. She had knelt down to look closer and smelled the sweet nectar mixed with decomposition and she was so sad and she dug a hole with her fingers, ripping the tip of her nail off and dug and dug until her fingerpads ached. She placed the little body of the bird onto a bed of grass, still wet with dew from the morning, and buried it, saying a small prayer and kissing the ground after patting down the dirt as hard as she could, pressing the weight of her body down to make sure that it never got dug up again, so that the bird rested peacefully.

Beth sat up in bed and waited for her husband to come. She had left a message on his office phone on her way over, letting him know that it was time; that their son would be born soon. She called again and told his secretary to make sure he gets the message. Beth looked around the room, taking note of the ugly drawing of a large pink crocus on the wall under dusty glass. There was a massive rocking chair in the corner with a faded and worn out cushion on the seat. There was a crocheted sign that she couldn't make out from the other side of the room.

Sweat

Her baby shifted and Beth felt the labour start for the first time painfully. She was surprised, had thought that the low cramping she was feeling was about as much as she would get. But her mother had warned her of the pain and she felt prepared. She lay back and could not get comfortable. She began to count the contractions with the nurse when she returned. 1-2-3-4-5-6-7-8-9-10-11-12 and they would fade back into her body. Still seven minutes apart. *Sit tight,* the nurse told her brightly, *You still have a way to go my dear.* And she was right. When her husband arrived an hour later, she was still seven minutes apart, even though the intensity of the contractions were increasing. The pain was deep, low in her back and she gritted her teeth as her husband watched her.

"How are doing, dear?" the short nurse with the dark hair asked, smiling a distracted but kind smile.

"Oh, it is very painful, much worse now than before."

"Sometimes if you walk, it could speed things up. It's worth a try to go up and down the hall. Gravity and the motion work wonders."

"I'll try. I really will. Give me a few minutes."

The contraction passed and Beth put on her slippers and opened the door to her room. She saw the other woman sharing the labour room slowly walk down the hallway, her arm pressed into her back, looking serious and steady, walking, walking. Beth's husband walked beside her, silent, slightly worried and looking tired.

"This is taking longer than I'd thought," Beth let her husband know.

"Don't worry, everything will take place as it's supposed to." He followed her slowly down the hallway.

The hospital was ugly. Chipped blue paint and scuffed walls. She knew they were planning on building a new hospital in the near future. It would have to be better than this. She remembered the General Hospital as a girl and it still looked the same. She was born in the Plummer Hospital next door, but that had since closed its doors on labour and delivery. It would have been nice to have her child in the same hospital. Beth passed a window and saw the view of the St. Mary's River. The river ran slowly, slight ripples billowing overtop like a simmering pot of water. The day was turning into night and there was a pink hue to the air. She could remember her mother looking out of the square kitchen window announcing *Red sky at night sailor's delight. Red sky in the morning, sailor's warning.* She remembered feeling afraid when the sky was reddened in the morning and always felt as though something ominous was waiting.

There were women everywhere and Beth was surprised by the number of women waiting for their new babies to be born the same day as her. She felt connected somehow to these women and tried to make eye contact with the others as they slowly walked the hallway, bellies swaying, legs thick and veiny under the blue hospital robes. There was a girl so young that Beth felt sorry for her. No more than sixteen, her belly seemed too large for the rest of her body. Her eyes were red from crying and her mother was beside her, frantic, trying to smile, her lips quivering, trying to soothe her with a hand on her hair that the girl kept pushing away.

While Beth watched her, another contraction overcame her and she gritted her teeth, anticipating the waves that hardened her belly into a great mass, lifting it and tensing her legs, and she held her breath, the pain rushing through her and holding her in its grasp while her husband whispered *Breathe Beth, don't hold your breath. The nurse said to breathe, remember. Breathe through it, in and out, just breathe.* His voice irritated her and she tried to block it out but it kept interfering and she placed her hands on the wall over a zigzagged crack and tried to breathe but couldn't, tried to push the air out in a great breath but couldn't, and she felt her face reddening and a pulse starting in her ears, and finally the breath came out in a rush and the contraction ebbed and the worldsounds came back into focus and she loosened her body and lifted a hand to wipe the sweat from her temple, a tear from the corner of her eye.

"I'm trying, honey, I'm really trying," Beth breathed.

"Okay, okay, let's continue walking," her husband whispered, looking nervously at her.

They walked for two hours until Beth was tired. Her legs shook and she was feeling irritable and impatient with the short, distracted nurse who kept peeking in briefly.

"I will check you now," the nurse stated, matter of fact, looking at her watch and into the hallway behind her. "Now, lie down and lift your legs."

Beth lay down on the hard mattress, hearing the plastic ripple under the starched sheet. The sound grated on her nerves and she missed her own bed, the soft air-blown sheets and the smell of morning on them. She missed the warmth of her caramel walls and hated these blue walls and the sight of the black night behind the flowered curtains. It was so hot in here and she wanted a drink of water. Her tongue was dry and her throat hurt from tensing up.

"Okay, now relax," the nurse ordered.

"I'm trying to relax, believe me, I really am," Beth told the nurse, clutching her husband's hand that was so cold inside of Beth's hot flesh.

The nurse put on a pair of gloves and squirted a glob of Vaseline onto the fingertips of the glove.

"Take a breath and relax now."

She adjusted her glasses with her other hand and leaned in, inserting two fingers, pushing them inward toward the opening of the cervix and finding it, stretching the opening painfully, feeling for the progress of the labour. The pain was overwhelming, a dark-hued rush of pain that made Beth yell out and whimper. The nurse felt the cervix with her fingertips and pushed her small hand inward deeply, twisting her hand around to feel deeper.

"I would say you are about six centimetres dilated now. Just about six. The cervix is still a bit thick. A way to go yet," the nurse stated thoughtfully.

"A way to go? Just six? But how is that possible? I've been walking. I've been here for hours. My contractions are coming so hard. I mean, I have to be more than that!" Beth cried, tears running down her cheeks.

"This is normal. This is your first birth. Sometimes it is the longest. This is to be expected." The nurse took off the gloves and tossed them into the nearby garbage can.

"I can't believe it," Beth moaned.

"Well, believe it and try to relax. It's getting late, now maybe try to get some sleep. You've got a long way to go and need your strength." The nurse smiled stiffly and went out the door, leaving Beth alone with her husband.

He sighed and sat down on the rocking chair. "Wow. It's going to be a long night. I thought for sure the baby'd be here tonight. I'm going to have to call the office and let them know I won't be in tomorrow."

"Well, maybe not. You never know." Beth turned to her side, feeling hopeless, guilty, angry, and impatient, dreading the next contraction. "Just try to sleep yourself."

Her husband sighed and closed his eyes and fell asleep within minutes.

For the next six hours, Beth rolled over and over trying to get comfortable, watching her husband sleep soundly, gritting her teeth, praying, wishing for her mother and her sisters, praying and calling the baby's name over and over: *DanielDanielDaniel, just come soon, just come, I want you, DanielDanielDaniel... Neegoosis, Neegoosis.*

At one o'clock the next afternoon, Beth still hadn't slept. She had been laboring here for over twenty-four hours and her waters still hadn't broken; she was exhausted and she was feeling worn out and hopeless. Her husband paced the floor, his suit wrinkled, his tie on the floor, his face looking desperate. Beth couldn't look at him and she was in agony, so tired that she was seeing yellow spots, so restless but in so much pain that she didn't want to move and wanted to bite into something to distract herself from the torrents of contractions that dug into her like a nightmare, that came fast and hard and frantic.

In the middle of it was a storm, lashes of currents into her lower back, a burning, a driving force monstrous in its growing, a fury of whipping branches, hail onto the skin, a gnashing of the organs, death in small pieces. She whimpered and sounded childish. Her husband paced, nurse stood expressionless and she screamed silently, the pounding in her ears a painful sound like an alarm that would not end. Her nails cut open her palmflesh. She did not feel it, just wanted it all to stop. Her husband spoke to the nurse about an epidural and she let him know that the doctor would inform the anesthesiologist and he would come in to speak to Beth. Labour had been going on so long that Beth felt distant from her own body, apart from every living thing in the world. She had not wanted an epidural, had refused pain medications and now she wondered why she would do such a thing.

"You don't have anything to prove Beth," her husband told her. "You aren't superwoman, that's for sure. Everyone gets an epidural."

But she had wanted to experience this birth fully. "I know, but…" She stopped to take a breath.

Her husband continued. "I mean, you always think you have to do everything just perfect. Not everything is set in stone. Decisions are meant to be changed."

Who was this man? Beth watched him from inside of her bubble of anguish and for a moment couldn't quite recollect where they'd met and why she had married him. His pacing unnerved her and his voice felt unfamiliar and foreign. What drew her to him in the first place? These questions came at her like a rainstorm and she dodged them, her mind an umbrella because she couldn't answer any of them, did not know how. She did not know him, not really. He was perfect. Flexed, poised, controlled. All effortlessly. Never a break in his calm, never out of place or late or rumpled. He didn't believe in spontaneity or walking around naked or skinny-dipping or rolling on the grass, two people in love, a little sun on their faces, laughing. His decisions never changed; he was stone, set perfectly, formed before he met her, etched finely and chiseled from a hand she did not understand.

And she collapsed on the floor and her husband's shoes were near her face and he was speaking to her and she ignored him and let herself be lifted, her body spasming from the pain of the baby's head pressed against her cervix, fighting to be released, her body resisted, his voice like a robot, his head and the nurse's together watching her like she is crazy, like she doesn't understand what they are saying, his lips barely moving when he speaks and the nurse nodding and nodding. Beth's body was drumming itself and she entered a different form of living, a wide space above her that she never knew was there, a reprieve, a grayness that was somehow welcoming in its thickness, a deserted embrace where she escaped from their voices, the blue chipped paint, the dreadful flowered curtains, and began to breathe deeply, lungs filling effortlessly, their voices drifting like water lilies or a pieces of birchbark floating upstream, a capsule of solitude where nothing else existed but her body, her baby's release and a small piece of driftwood being carefully and flawlessly whittled into creation, perfect and small and smelling of new sweat, steam, salt and desire unleashed. His voice tired and persistent, begging her to *let go let go*, his voice a crooked pathway making her trip and stumble, the hollow path bringing her to her knees, but they keep pulling at her, pulling her down this path, forcing her to walk, walk, walk, the way a child might walk a doll while playing.

They walked her to the delivery room, hands on either side of her, balancing her. She was steady even though there was an intense pressure between her thighs and she felt like pushing, pushing, like expelling the heaviness that was bearing down on her, a natural inclination to push until she cannot breathe to combine her strength and will and pain to bear down and growl and paw at the ground and eat the plants at her lips and to not care who is watching and to release this baby from her cervix which she felt was open now to allow the passing of one lifesource to their own and to die trying if she had to, to die trying if need be. She leaned into her husband's shoulder and pushed a little, not wanting the baby to fall to the floor and trying to hold it in all at once.

"What are you doing?" her husband asked. "Beth, for goodness sakes, continue walking. We're going to get you the epidural and then you'll be yourself."

"He's ready now. I feel him coming."

"The nurse says you have a ways to go yet. You were only seven centimetres last time we checked and that was only about a half hour ago. You're not fully dilated or effaced. You can walk, or I can get one of those chairs over there and push you." He pointed to a rusting wheelchair in the corner.

Again she looked at him and this time she couldn't talk and she was glad she couldn't because if she could, she would grab the collar of his ironed shirt and tear it and bare her teeth at him and laugh at his knowledge of her body, but she could not, and she was glad. Her husband leaned into the nurse in front of her and they conspired about the wheelchair, nodding, nodding. Her husband decided to grab it and Beth collapsed into it, nudged by the graying nurse with her serious eyes and nametag that read *Sheila.* She collapsed into it, leaning back, feeling something like drifting mixed with fear into adrenaline.

Beth felt a strange lifting sensation of collapsing into this reality and drifting upward into the gray space and could not choose which path to take, so she chose both and sat in the wheelchair, seeing every crack in the wall, but watching from above at the same time and she accepted this and knew that in minutes she would exhale and her son would be born and this would all be worth it and she could not wait and she pushed and they both looked at her telling her to *wait, wait, wait, we're almost there* and she pushed, her lips opening and she howled, a sound that turned all heads her ways as she arched her back and thrust her hips forward and felt her legs go taut with the effort, a watersplash in her ears and she watched from above, her long hair wet with sweat, her hands that gripped the metal railings of the wheelchair, her fingers white with pressure and the pushing, the pushing a relief, a long-awaited gift and she smiled from above and she grunted down below and before she returned to the physical, she saw the long tuft of black hair jutting out from under her blue-printed hospital gown, soft and so pure and she screamed one long and winding wail that sounded like falling in her ears, a rushing that did not end.

20

Jolene

JOLENE LEAVES THE SWEAT QUICKLY, puke everywhere, down her new jeans, over her shirt and her hands. She breathes in the night air, gulping it down like water and it is cold and fiery, almost painful. So dark, she stumbles over a long root, but makes it up the hill toward the healing lodge where the bathrooms are. *Shit,* she thinks, *and I wasn't even drinking. Maybe I'm coming down with something.* The lights are on in the healing lodge and it is nice and cool inside. Jolene goes into the bathroom and looks at herself in the mirror. She looks okay, a little puffy from crying, a little shiny from sweating. Her hair sticks to the back of her neck hotly. She washes her hands and gets paper towels and begins to scrub the puke from her shirt and pants as best as she can. She rinses her mouth out and starts to feel a bit better. She notices her hands are shaky. She leans her head against the paper towel holder and tries to breathe in and out slowly, the images of the last half hour shooting through her head.

She doesn't notice Elsa come into the washroom and she jumps when she feels the hand on her arm.

"Geez, you scared me," Jolene whispers, fear in her voice.

"I know, I'm pretty scary looking, eh?" Elsa laughs that long laugh that Jolene finds pleasant and familiar.

"I was just lost in thought there."

"You don't have to whisper."

"Yeah, I guess you're right. I just feel, well, I feel..." She pauses.

"Don't worry, I understand," Elsa says. "I can still remember the first sweat I went into. You know, I didn't stay as long as you. Too hot. Too intense."

"You know, it wasn't really the heat. Not really. I mean the heat was intense, for sure. I felt sometimes I couldn't even breathe. It's a thick heat, eh? That's how I can describe it." Jolene drifts off.

"Yes, thick. Good choice of word. Thick and deep. The heat penetrates the flesh. But, if you noticed, even more than that." Elsa observes Jolene.

"I noticed, trust me. I feel kind of, well, not nervous, hmm... how do I say it. I guess I'm just not used to trying to describe my feelings. I find it hard. Kind of weird I guess." Jolene looks down.

"Come on, let's go sit around the firepit in the lodge. It's not too comfortable standing here in the bathroom, is it?" Elsa laughs.

Jolene looks around, as though she forgot where she was. "Oh yeah, we're in the bathroom, aren't we?"

"Even though my old man says I spend more time in the bathroom than anywhere else, especially kitchen!" Elsa laughs again as she turns and leads Jolene out of the bathroom toward the round pit of rocks and logs in the healing lodge.

"Wow," breathes Jolene, "It's really beautiful in here. It smells good too." She takes a deep breath.

They both sit at the edge of the firepit and look around. The ceiling is high and pointed upward, long logs leading up to the peak. The smell of cedar permeates the air and even though the fire is not lit at the moment, a smoky aroma hangs inside the lodge. There are several carved, wooden benches around the circle, and paintings by local artists like John LaFord and Peter Migwans. There is an office off to the side and a long kitchen in the back. On the sides, there are several rooms with bunks inside as sleeping quarters for those travelling through, or for those on a healing quest who need time away in order to heal here at the lodge. The sound of birds comes through the open doors, a scurrying of brush, a distant shriek of an owl.

"And to answer your question, no," Elsa tells Jolene.

"No what?"

"No, it is not weird to find it hard to describe your feelings. That is completely normal. I think we all find it hard." Elsa nods, running a trail of rocks over the tips of her toes.

"Really?" Jolene asks her. "You seem like the type to be able to know exactly what you feel and exactly what you want."

Elsa laughs again and the sound echoes through the empty room. "Oh, and there's a type for that, huh?"

"Well, I guess what I mean is that you seem confident. And you seem very peaceful. Only someone who has dug through their big well of feelings and discovered that they like what they find there is usually so happy and peaceful."

"Well, thanks, I guess, for the compliment." Elsa looks at Jolene. "Yes, I do feel confident. And I do feel very peaceful lately. But I didn't always. Not at all. I've been through hard times, like anyone else, and I had to go to my past to uncover a lot of these things. I had to pull them out like a dirty pile of laundry, examine them, see which ones were worst, start washing them by hand, little bits at a time, ring them out, hang them to dry, and then when

I took them down and examined them again, I realized some were clean and some were still dirty!"

"But why would they still be dirty if you washed them?" Jolene asks.

"Well, some of them had years and years of buildup. Decades of stains and filth and dirt. I had to wash those ones ten, twenty, thirty times before most of it came off. And honestly, some of it still has stains and dirt." Elsa nods.

"Yeah, I get it."

"Do you?" Elsa continues. "You see, healing is a process. A long one. It's not easy, not something you do in a day. Or a month. Or even a year. Sometimes not even in a decade. And for many people, a lifetime."

"A lifetime? Really?"

"Could be. Becoming who our Creator wants us to be can be a process, right?" Elsa looks at Jolene. "Hard in the beginning. Believe me. But it does get easier and easier. Especially once you start looking at the world in a new way and start seeing things like it's the first time."

"What do you mean?" Jolene asks. She's not sure she likes the direction this is going.

"After the painful initial sloughing off of the first layer of dirt, you feel lighter, more positive, like something literally has been lifted off your being. I kid you not." Elsa laughs. "Well, at least that is how it was for me."

"Yeah, but your dirt was probably cleaner than mine!" Now Jolene laughs, and realizes that it sounds fake and she feels a lump rise in her throat and she thinks that if she doesn't laugh she will cry.

"Jolene, listen." Elsa looks concerned. "Healing is good thing. And for goodness sakes, all dirt is dirty."

Sweat

"Yeah, but you...you seem so...good." Jolene shrugs and looks down.

"And dammit, I *feel* good. Real good. I take care of myself now. You know, it took me almost till I was 35 before I laughed a real laugh. I'm not joking. I never smiled as a kid. Never. I sure never laughed."

"Why not? You don't have a problem with it now!" They both laughed.

"That's for sure, isn't it? I have to make up for all the laughs I lost."

"Well, tell me why," Jolene asks simply.

Elsa pauses, runs pebbles over her toes, looks up and breaths deep. "Maybe someday I'll spill all the sordid details for you. But not now. The quick version is that I was a drinker, like my dad. By the time I was a teenager we were regular lushes, one minute each other's favourite person, the next whaling on each other—blood and snot everywhere. I alienated most of my family, especially my innocent little sister, who witnessed a lot of it. I still remember the look on her face, of shock and shame—it made me want to run away. Lookin' at her made me see my own monstrosity. God, how I loved her and hated myself. It's hard to love someone so completely and be so lost and doing hateful things. The blend of the two is too guilt-filled, too truthful."

Jolene feels something close to understanding.

"So I left. I went to college somehow, had a baby that was normal somehow, hid it all somehow for a long, long time. But, I did quit eventually. I quit for my daughter and I quit for myself. And for the man who loved me through the end of it and for some crazy reason still does. I am still fighting with the dirt, the scrubbing of my soulskins, but it is happening, that's for sure. I can sit here and talk to you and not fear all that goodness I see in you."

"In me? You've got to be kidding." Jolene shrugs. "But thanks for saying so. I feel like the old you."

"We probably all do sometimes. But I don't think that's the real us. It's just the part of us that hides, that we create to hide behind. I used the drunk me as a protection against what I was really supposed to be. I didn't want to feel the pain. I expect we all want to hide from our hurts. Listen to me, soundin' like a preacher. But hey, you're a good girl, anyone can see that."

"Well, maybe I'll see it someday. I know I felt some weird things in that sweat, things I've never felt before."

"Well, keep on facing them. It can be scary, but the end result is worth it. To start living life is worth it. And don't worry, I'll be here to listen if you need to talk."

"But why would you help me?" Jolene asks, confused by Elsa's offer of friendship. "You don't even know me."

"Because that's what friends are for and I want to be your friend. People are put in front of each other to help each other. I see a girl who needs someone and I used to be that girl wishing that someone was there to stand by me when I needed it. That's why. A simple enough reason, but the truth. So if you ever want to take me up on it, I'm always here. I work in that office and you just come here or call me."

"Okay, I'll remember that."

The women stand and laugh when they realize that their legs are numb.

"Geez, I have an excuse," Elsa laughs, "I'm old. What's your excuse?" They head outside to breathe in the cool air.

Jolene laughs too, admiring the night sky.

21

The Grandmothers

THE GIRL ROSE. HER MOTHER STOOD BESIDE HER, arm on arm, fingers that sturdied her, held her in a delicate balance while her legs shook, weak from the weeks of lying. The girl's legs stepped twice and then wavered, much like a fawn, legs skinnied and brown. One of the grandmothers came forward and helped the mother lead her daughter across the floor, slowly, while the other women stood nearby in case they needed to jump in to help, the girl's babies watching their own mother's struggle into movement, desperate to regain a lost strength. The girl inhaled the smells of the air, the tobacco, the sage, the long pull of yarrow and willed it to seep into her pores, enter her throat and begin its work on her. She saw yellowed dots behind her eyes and forced the steps, fighting against the will to fall, a desire to drop to the floor and sleep some more, just sleep a deep sleep of the dying.

The girl's mother worried for her daughter. Her milk was dried up and she could not sit to feed her own babies. Her grandchildren suckled happily from another of the mothers, sharing her own child's milk with the twins. The women lay the babies down beside the girl while she slept and they leaned against the warmth of her breast and sometimes slept, and sometimes stared at the sky of faces always above them, touching them, rubbing oils on their skins, singing songs that melted into their consciousness like a sap down the edge of the side of a fat maple. The babies thrived, grew bigger, faces rounding, small moons that gurgled while they observed their world of women, two boys who fell in love with all, not knowing which one was their mother, not caring, just enjoying the hands and voices and beat of a handdrum through the days and nights.

When the girl rose, the two small faces turned to her, seeing the long black hair like all of the other women, falling over her shoulders, half-hiding her own face, so thin that her clothing fell off her shoulder, exposing a jutting bone that fell as sharply as the rock edges of Agawa, grey and flat and hard as time itself. The boys barely blinked as she walked, just watched the girl step slowly and pant loudly, the sounds puffing forward into the morning, a sound that mesmerized the babies, quieted them. When she was carried back to her low bed of skins and furs, they closed their eyes and dreamed of the feel of warm flesh against their cheek, the joy of a nipple on their lips, the hot gush of milk running over the silky inner flesh of their cheeks. Their hands found each other and rested against the other, happy to be laid together, little bodies pressed side by side, one so dark and the other as pale as one of the white men that sometimes passed through, that watched them with their mouths open, curious, awed by their ways, not blinking until they looked away, until the teepees disappeared into the bush behind them, their horses' hoofs pounding against the cooled autumn dirt.

Sweat

The girl leaned her head against her headrest of furs and was relieved to be back down to the ground. She peeked at her babies, two blurs of brown and pink, and she smiled, the sight of their chubby bodies delighting her, creating a peace deep inside her, her weakness taking over, new blood slowly leaking from between her legs, and she slept some more, her life paused, all thoughts blank behind the empty dreams, the pure white vision that she sees while she sleeps, comforting her in its lack of persistence, its complete and uninterrupted silence.

22

Beth

WHEN DANIEL DID NOT WAKE UP after his surgery, Beth fell to the ground in one motion, but the falling persisted into weeks, the dizziness, the vertigo, a feeling that she was no longer on the ground, that she was flying and would never reach bottom. She remembered the doctor's hands, thinking they were strong and clean with nails so clipped and perfect, and that these hands would bring her baby back to her, wrapped and cleaned and sleeping the sleep of all perfect babies.

When they took him from her body she could not touch him, he was pulled from her in one giant gulp, the sound was immense, a massive thrust that shook the whole world, a breaking apart that wrenched her with its completion, a split that ripped her at the seams, body and soul, one long jagged tear. Without his movements inside of her, Beth felt incomplete, without his tight wriggling, her stomach hung loosely, deflated and emptied, her purpose served, and a loneliness for his small body within her permeated every second of her until she touched him again, felt his small, new flesh under her fingers.

When she held him, it was only for a moment until they had him bundled and whisked into a helicopter to the Sick Kids Hospital in London, Ontario. She was wheeled to the doorway and waddled to the helicopter doors and they flew quickly, and she did not sleep again, never slept a perfect sleep again because his whimpers, the baby cry, followed her for the next two years, long after she buried him, long after her body healed and she roamed her empty house, the nursery which she cleared out and packed away, long after her husband slept and she stared at the shadows on the walls as the cars drove by, months and years and minutes and it all blended into one long cry, a strong, pungent birthcry, as sharp as lightning and as endless as a perfect circle, round and round and round.

People called and Beth spoke to them. She heard her voice steady and calm, she heard her words and did not understand them. Her instincts still whispered *DanielDanielDanielwhereare youwhereareyou?* But she knew where he was but she still felt his presence on everything, every program on TV, every birdcall, every stranger pushing a baby carriage and she grew angry with these women who walked so casually, who did not grab their babies and hold onto them so tight and never let go, just let them lie there in their strollers while they walked, chatting everyday things to the women walking beside them. She felt like taking these women by the arms and shaking them and screaming at them and lifting their babies into their arms and feeling the warmth of their tiny backs beneath her arms and loving them for a minute until she would look down and the face wouldn't be his, would never be his, would never be her son's again.

Her husband did not weep at the funeral. She never saw him waver from his strength, from his eternal calm and she could not reach out and touch him, could not share her amount of grief with him. She wanted the coffin closed, did not want to see his face like this, did not want his death to be the last time she saw him, wanted to remember seeing his small mouth screaming after they cut the cord, wanted to remember the stretch of his lips that held his scream, the life that flowed there, the small and long limbs that moved and kicked when lifted, the black of his hair that was jutting out beneath the birthfluids, the blood.

She went home that day and stayed in bed for months. Her sisters came and sat beside her, fed her, opened the windows for her. She remembers the sight of their hands on their laps beside her bed. She could not look up to their faces, did not want to see any faces with their sad eyes, the worry there that she was causing, the pain. But their hands were never still, wringing each other, sweaty, nervous movements that made her feel like dying too, made her feel like just slipping away to be with Daniel. She knew her body was somehow responsible for this, her insides, her selfishness, something about her caused this and she felt like a monster, an indescribable animal, the kind that is wild and eats her young and swallows and swallows and swallows hungrily, eyes roving.

She slept for a long time and soon it was winter and they told her it was a cold one and they piled her with blankets and blankets of bright colours to make her happy and put her paintings on her walls and she did feel happy sometimes with all of these colours and her memories and the hum of her sisters' voices colliding. When she rose, many hands guided her and she sat at her kitchen table, feeling like a stranger in this house and a traitor for living and breathing and wanting to be fed, wanting to be a part of the cooking and preparing and to feel her sisters' hands on hers and know that she is loved, accepted.

His leaving his squirm out the powerful thrust he made through the tunneling his strength the squished determination on his face, the way his fists balled until the edges were white under the bloodmarks. His little fists opening and closing, his little fists wrestling with life, his little fists so small that they looked like little red salmon mouths opening and closing. His eyes sealed shut by blood. His eyes forcing their lids open. His eyes pushing through the layers of grime and finding the light and his hands never stopped moving. They moved and they worked. His fingers worked and knew what it felt like to open and close the air in his palm. He knew how to work his body open to life. He knew and I saw him. I saw his desperation to live, to hold life in those small palms. The lines of his palms filled with my bodyblood. I should have moved my face so he could see me. I should have moved my hand to be in his those seconds when his hands were trying to hold permanence. Their hands holding me down, the doctors lifting his body away from me. My body emptied and he was gone so fast.

Beth's husband's workload increased after the death of their baby. He began to work all the time, coming home to shower and sleep. She sometimes wondered if he ate during the day, but did not begin to cook. She didn't ask him. Their bodies sometimes met, by choice, by accident, but their eyes rarely did, and she knew that she wanted him still, craved his body and his heat on his side of the bed, unmoving and still, his features softened by sleep, his small breaths gentle and good and quiet.

It was hard to dream and her dreams were sliced apart, broken and fragmented liked whittled wood, chipped and drifting into the air, lost to the carver's hand. Long after her mother and sisters left for their own homes, their own lives, Beth would wake up in the night, sweating and heart racing, feeling trapped and cemented into her bed, unable to move. Finally her limbs would edge out of their heaviness and she would stretch them outward, her eyes on her husband's back, the long curve of it, and wonder where he went when he dreamed, where his mind took him, and knowing that she would never know. And the crying did not stop, and some nights it took on a howling sound, like a baby in distress and she, like a novice mother, pacing the floor, not knowing what to do to quell the sounds. Trees whipped against the house and these midnight sounds stayed for years, coloured her nights like a long, black stroke of a paintbrush, that only consisted of grays, browns, and blacks, stroking loudly against her heart.

One day, Beth left the house, took a walk and the earth felt different to her. She noticed things she did not before, gutters filled with waste, cigarette butts littering the sidewalks and long cracks on pavement. Everything was uglier, less humane, and brutal to her eyes. She missed the safety of her home, its neatness, the curved staircase and elegant lines of wood on the floors. She missed the smells of safety in creased laundry and freshly cleaned silverware from a hot dishwasher, its steam clouding her face like a long sagewind, smudging her pores from the inside out. She sighed and hurried on, knowing she had to breathe in the outside, knowing her legs needed the stretch of exercise, her lungs a different pull of air. She felt lonely on these walks that soon became a ritual, felt old against the young mothers out strolling their babies to sleep, felt hopeless with no one to walk behind her, no stroller to push, no husband to hold hands with.

The third year, Beth turned down her street onto Queen Street and walked all the way downtown, past Algoma University, past Bellevue Park, past the Buglab, past all of the shops and dentist offices, to a small office she read about in a small ad in the newspaper, to a woman whose name she already knew was Dorothy Parsons, to her long desk and let her know that she wanted to be a foster mother to a baby as soon as possible. Beth had read an article the month before about the need for foster parents in the Sault Ste. Marie area, specifically for Aboriginal children. Dorothy looked at Beth and asked her questions and Beth answered them, her voice steady, her resolve firm. She made an appointment the following week to come in and fill out the forms and allow the service to do the appropriate checks needed.

And please, Beth mentioned, I would prefer a Native boy, if possible, as I can teach him our culture and be an appropriate role model for him.

She felt her chin lifting and falling, nodding and smiling. She left the office and walked home, shaking with excitement, knowing that she would never have another baby of her own, and feeling for the first time okay with that possibility. She would talk to her husband later that night to let him know of her wishes, let him know the need for a child in the house, of her heart about to burst if she couldn't love a baby, have a little hand in hers, of her readiness to let her heart slip into another and stay there. *If not, she would tell him, I might as well die. I might as well have died with Daniel. Did I die with him? Is this me walking here? What am I doing?*

It was night when she came back home, nightfall, and the house was as empty as a tomb, her husband nowhere in sight, no shoes by the door, no note, just a big, empty house, its silence as quick as a punch, the sound of her footsteps echoing loudly as she felt her way through the darkness to her room to collapse into her bed, unwashed, shoes still on, craving sleep so deeply that she was dizzy. All went black and she slept the full night through, and woke the next day quieted, a small smile on her lips, feeling rested for the first time in years.

23

Jolene

JOLENE DROVE HER AUNTIE'S CAR to the edge of town just outside
of Garden River to a small motel right at the city limits, got herself
a weekly rate with the last of her money and sat on the edge of the
flower-patterned bedspread, tiredness and satisfaction coursing
through her. She was thrilled that she made it through the sweat,
and even though so many of the experiences were confusing,
she already wanted to go again, and to see Elsa again. She was so
different than Jolene's usual friends, so much more serious and
serene, but Jolene didn't mind, in fact she wanted that difference;
it made her feel more grounded, happier. She looked around the
room, sighed and wished she had more money so she could order
a pizza, some wings and have a nice cold ginger ale. That was okay.
She could go days without eating and still feel strong. She took the
plastic wrapper from a solid glass cup and filled it up three times
with lukewarm tap water, gulping thirstily, not realizing that she

was so thirsty. She washed her face with the small rectangular bar of hardened soap which barely lathered and she dried her face with the towel on the plastic rack, its texture scratching her face like granules of sand.

Jolene peeled off her jeans and top, pulled the bedspread back and crawled onto the squeaky bed between the sheets like looked whiter and cleaner than she expected to find. She felt renewed and she knew that she would sleep well. She had no desire to call her friends to see if there was a party or something going on. After all, it was only eleven o'clock and the night was still young. But she felt different, still a bit dizzy from the intense heat; she felt peaceful and she wanted to think about the sweat, about her new friend, Elsa, and all of the feelings that she felt inside the structure of women she'd found herself in that evening.

She felt strange being back in this area, outside of Toronto where she could always hide herself if she wanted to, remain anonymous, but she needed to be here for a bit to check things out, see what she found and revisit her past, which she had forgotten for so long. She knew her Auntie wouldn't mind if she kept the car for a week, just as long as she gave her a call the next day to let her know she would be a little bit longer than expected. She wondered if she'd run into anybody she knew, but she didn't think so because she'd been so young, but she knows her mama had family in Garden River and had many friends who might remember the little girl with the long, black hair always by her mama's leg, holding on for dear life.

Jolene reached over and turned off the bedside light and lay on the bed watching the lights from the passing cars fall onto the wall and foot of the bed. A train sped by and the memory of the traintracks from her childhood rushed through her, the way the house actually shook with each passing train, and she remembered liking the vibrations, the feeling that people were zooming by, that life was in motion and that the world would still go on without anybody knowing that she and her mama were asleep in the bush, in their little brown house that blended into the night, their breaths making no difference to the world at all, the sound of them almost nothing at all, like the crawl of a ladybug on a leaf, or the turn of a muskrat watching the world around it.

She fell into sleep easily. Jolene was never afraid to be alone, never afraid to sleep in the darkness or walk down the streets alone. She craved the quiet always; even in the middle of a loud party, voices moving like storm currents, she found her niche in her thoughts, in the low drum of herself, the quiet space of her mind where nobody entered but memory, the drift of the past so ever-present and familiar. Sometimes a friend would poke her arm, laughing at her, dragging her back to the present. Someone always shaking her, poking at her, reminding her that she was still alive. And she would smile and laugh and talk and say all of the things she was supposed to say to let everyone know that she was there.

The sleep is thick, comes at her like a sudden fog and she falls into it fast. Running through the fog she sees faces, limbs, hears voices and she runs faster, trying to avoid contact, trying to find a crevice to fall into to escape everyone and to scurry down into to hibernate the years away like a skinnied bear, exhausted from the years past, ready for a long, undisturbed rest. Jolene stops when she sees long hair falling over a face. She knows her mama without having to see her face. She knows the shape of her neck, the long fall of her arms outside of her sleeves, the arc of her back as she leans forward. She pulls in her breath, awed by her mama, amazed at the burst of love that gushes out of her that she thought was gone, a yearning for the thin hands around her, a need for her mama's soft words, a glimpse of her face. Just one minute alone with her to touch her face, bury her face in her hair, to smell the perfume and smoke, to breathe again, to live again, makes Jolene step forward, arms out: *Mama? Mama?*

Her mama looks up, hand in mid-strum, her guitar open on her lap and she smiles the smile that opens childhood's seams, unstitches the bindings and weavings and lets Jolene's soul flow to the feet of her mama.

My girl. You've come.

Mama, mama.

The feel of their skins colliding, the hearts of the two women meeting causes Jolene to gasp, to taste the colour of their loss, to hear the years weeping for them and she looks up into her mama's eyes, unable to ask the questions that have been plaguing her for so many years, unable to speak.

Jolene, I've never left you. I've been with you every second.

Her mama's hands against her cheeks, those hands that sounds like grass in mid-growth, the coolness, a water over her, washing.

And I am so proud. My baby girl. I have loved your every footstep, your every breath and I have cried all of those tears that you've held inside. I have cried them for you so they don't drown you.

Mama?

I know. I know where you've been, where you've had to go. Did you ever feel me stroking your hair? Whispering to you? My baby, I've never stopped crying since we parted. I've never taken my eyes from you.

But, mama?

My girl, they are beautiful and they look like you, every inch of them.

Mama?

When you screamed, I took your pain and I swallowed it and took it from you. I wished I could have held them, been beside you through it all.

But, they are...

You don't need to say it, I know, I know.

You do?

You know I do.

And…?

I love you so much. My heart aches with my love for you.

Where…?

You saw me in their eyes, didn't you? It scared you at first, just for a second when you thought you saw my eyes. Well, you did. I am there, and you are too. We will pass on for generations.

I… I'm…

Shhh… sweetheart, you did good. You are so good, like the inside of the first buds, the way they are nestled there inside of their wrapping, just waiting for spring where they will bloom and let their petals lie open for the whole world to see. That is you, my girl. You are so beautiful, so much like the person I knew you'd be the first time I ever held you. The day you were born I knew that you were good, much better than anything I'd ever seen, much better than I could have ever dreamed of being. And when you looked at them, you saw the same thing, didn't you? Didn't you see the greatest thing that you ever saw?

Yes mama, yes.

So, now, go in peace. I must go too. You first. I want to watch you run, your hair flying behind you, the same as when you were five running through the field. My girl, I love you.

No, mama. Wait.

Listen, go. I will watch you. Go my girl. Run. Maajaan. Maajaan.

Jolene runs, the wind lifting her and carrying her to a great field, her legs thumping against the night wind, a pattering that sounds like a guitar so fine-tuned that the stars stand to attention, the moon sharpens and the whole world arches to hear the sound. Above her, the sky opens and a great root grows downward, curling together as a hand with many fingers curled around the whole of the earth.

When she awoke, Jolene knew why she had come back to the reserve, to the Sault Ste. Marie area. For the first time, she knew.

136

24

The Grandmothers

THE FIRST MONTH INTO THE WINTER, the grandmothers knew that the girl was preparing to leave. Her legs had grown strong again, the bleeding was completely gone, and the girl's body had regained its muscle, the long shape of its health, lean and strong. She sipped her tea and held her babies tightly. There were tears in her eyes as she stared into the eyes of her boys, stroked the sides of their soft cheeks that were so plump from the milk, the moose broth, the many hands that caressed them to sleep each night. The eyes watched their mother, observed her tears and tried to reach up and touch the beautiful face with the long, earth-coloured eyes.

Neegoosis. Neegoosis. The girl's breath as water.

This water is sacred, she remembered from somewhere.

She knew the little brown eyes would follow her wherever she went, would stay with her during her travels, her life-journey, would keep her dreams filled each night, the memory of them. She knew also that they would be safe here with her women, the women she loved, her mother and sisters and aunts and grandmothers. She needed to go.

One final touch. *Neegoosis ag.* She passed the boys one by one to the waiting hands, the arrangement of hands in their stages of mothering, some old, some plump and young, some wrinkled and dry and some so soft that she thought of petals falling or raindrops in the morning, a slow descent that made her catch her breath in remembrance. She took it as a sign and stood. Her mother helped her stand, strong hands under her armpits, the scent of her breath filled with sumach, her cheek as warm as the first glint of fire, its wisp a stroke against the flesh, a medicine in itself.

Nimaamaa. She looked into her mother's face and the tears steady as her mother looked directly at her, into her. *Gimikwenden ina?* Yes nimaamaa, I remember.

Then go. Her mother said: *Maajaan. Maajaan.*

The girl squeezed her mother's hand, looked at the other women, saw her babies safe and wrapped in their arms and she turned to go.

Giga-waabamin-minawaa. The women nodded and extended their arms, offering her peace. The oldest grandmother stepped forward and handed her a moosehide sack filled with provisions for her journey. The girl took it and accepted the smoke twirling her way, inhaled it deeply and was warmed by the coursing into her lungs, her spirit.

25

Jolene

IT WASN'T HARD TO FIND OUT WHERE THEY WERE. She visited friends of her mother, she went to the official office of Family Services, and she talked to people, and soon enough, she knew of the whereabouts of the children. She drove by the house often, hoping for a glimpse, a quick peek, a long look at the two children that she knew were behind the walls of the big brick house and hedges that trailed the length of the driveway in the East End home in Sault Ste. Marie.

She was sure that maybe her Auntie had called the police. She had been over a week longer than she had told her Auntie that she'd be. She knew that her Aunt would need her car back sooner or later, that she would need to go out and do groceries, or go to an appointment or travel out of town. When she left, she promised to come back quickly with a full tank of gas, some money leftover for some portion of the rent, and when waving goodbye, she saw the uncertainty in her Auntie's eyes, but backed out anyway, tires squealing and dust lifting, blocking out the rearview mirror.

The drive to the Sault was great, the cities whipping by, Barrie, Parry Sound, French River, Sudbury, Blind River, Desbarats, St. Joe's Island, Echo Bay, and Jolene basked in the familiarity, the safety that she felt in the speed under the tires, the long trip homeward, the wind inching its way into the crack in the windows onto her forehead, all sound on the radio drowned out by the rush of wind. She felt alive and free, driving without anyone telling her where to go, stopping whenever she pleased, enjoying the flicker of a deer in the bush, a ripple of water on a passing creek.

When she came to the long bridge that said *This is Indian Land*, she knew she was home. When she passed by the band office, the old Catholic church on the highway, the sideroad where she grew up, she slowed the car, considered driving by the old house, but couldn't make her hands turn the wheel left to the entrance toward the point, so she continued driving. She stopped by the gas station that had been there for as long as she could remember, and she told the young girl to fill it up. She entered the station to pay and there was a tilted bulletin board with notices, rentals, cribs for sales, lost cats and a big white paper stapled to the board that said WOMAN'S SWEAT FRIDAY NIGHT, Healing Lodge, Garden River. Jolene knew it was Friday and she wondered where the healing lodge was, because it wasn't here when she lived here.

And she went and she was glad and she met Elsa and for some reason, after that sweat, she couldn't leave, couldn't make her feet push the pedal and hands turn back on that highway back to Toronto no matter how much she wanted to, no matter how hard she tried. The thought of going back to her Auntie's couch, her clothes in a Zehrs recyclable bag, her only pair of shoes by the front door, her pictures in a small box under her Auntie's organ in the

corner made her cringe just thinking about it. The nights with the
TV flashing blue against midnight's flat gaze on the faded paint of
the walls, the Kraft dinner, the parties with her buddies down the
hallway, the hangovers, the lonely walks down the street looking
at young mother's with their crisp shirts and shiny faces… and she
could not leave here if she tried. She could not go back to that life
that meant nothing all along, just biding time and taking space in
her Auntie's cramped apartment, pretending not to hear the nights
when Auntie sneaked her boyfriend in, feeling so intrusive and
huge on the couch, like an old nest half eaten by the winter, void of
birds, eggs, just pokey sticks that are pulled this way and that way
by a hungry wind.

She woke the second day in the motel thinking of the babies.
Remembering their faces side by side in a single crib, skins so soft
that she never wanted to touch them, thinking they might break
under her hard hand, her chipped nails and small ring that she
loved that belonged to her mother. But she touched them anyways,
stroked their cheeks while they slept, watched them, could not sleep
while they slept, wanting to absorb their beauty into her somehow,
knowing that she didn't deserve them, knowing how much better
they were than her, not fully believing that they were from her own
body. How could they be? How could these two beautiful little
boys with breath like dawn and fingers that moved like the first
break of creation come from her? She couldn't imagine how this
could be true, but she remembered the pushing, remembered the
heat in her back, the blood on her thighs, the instant shift from girl
to mother, their release as they slid from her, leaving her emptied,
alone, so alone in the dark room, her stomach deflated, her heart
heavy with love, so afraid for these babies, afraid of herself.

Fear gripped her as she watched the boys. Their mouths moved
like starving birds while they slept, their chests lifted and fell and

breath moved out of them. Their eyelids fluttered and she thought of hummingbird wings, late spring and the currents behind her mama's house under the wind. They were beautiful, one so dark, one pale, but their faces so alike. She was amazed and couldn't name them, couldn't pull her elders out of the woodwork and ask them for help, couldn't even call her auntie because she never told her she was pregnant.

Jolene, you are looking so sluggish. Let's have a walk.

Auntie, I'm tired. Must be coming down with something. I'm sorry, I am so tired, I just need to sleep.

You sleep so much. Are you okay?

Yes, yes. I will be fine. Just go. Go and walk, but I need to lie down a bit.

But the babies prospered inside of her. Lived and flourished inside of her scarred and weak flesh. Jolene didn't drink anymore and she threw her cigarettes out when she knew they were inside of her, not digging them back out even though she wanted to, wanted to pretend that they weren't there, but she couldn't. She loved the feeling of butterflies under her tummy, the flutterings, the sudden awakening as though she had been asleep for a long, long time and suddenly woke up, like she had been dead and now her flesh was fire, burning everything and everyone around her, but keeping her safe and warm, her babies safe, her babies warm.

And she was happy. Felt truly happy those nights, just her and the babies asleep under the blankets, rubbing her tummy, feeling the life that she was able to carry, her body expanding, hidden under sweaters and loose shirts and jogging pants. And nobody knew. Nobody knew. No one asked. Nobody noticed. But she knew. She remembered waking up one night in August knowing they were there under her skin, inside of her womb, just knowing it as clear as a voice. She was quiet. And happy. And so afraid, so afraid. Just kept quiet, growing so quietly, so silent that nobody asked and she didn't tell.

When the pains came she tried to ignore them as long as possible, tried to pace, tried to walk, tried to bathe it all away, but they were persistent and she borrowed her Auntie's car to go to the hospital.

I'm meeting friends. I'll be back tomorrow. Don't worry, I'll put some gas in the tank.

That's fine. I walk to work anyway. Take your time Jolene. You never go anywhere anymore. It'll do you good to go out with friends.

Thanks Auntie. Thanks.

And she went, the wheel clutched under her fingers so tightly that her knuckles were white, when she looked into the rear view mirror at herself, veins popped out of her forehead, her face purpling, breaths like punches filling the inside of the car, rhythmic, startling, like a series of quills smashing together, a fancydance that never ends. She parked and walked and collapsed on the front desk. They helped her to the room and she almost didn't make it. Her legs hoisted into silver stirrups, hands holding her legs apart and back and she felt taken over, apart from her own body, sweat soaking into her like rain, like a wave toppling her over, drowning her with its onslaught.

They came so quickly, furiously, like they wanted to burst out of her, like they wanted to escape from the confines of her flesh, that she felt abandoned, abandoned, left to bleed herself to sleep on the hard hospital bed, strange faces looking down at her, whispering: *Two big boys, strong boys, beautiful boys.*

So many hands lifting the bodies. Those fingers curled around them. And then offering them to her to be with, to press her cheeks to theirs. Hers shaky and their eyes finding hers their eyes moving to hers, small eyebrows bending in watchfulness. Watching her.

And when she held them and they were so perfect and they were so beautiful and they were so alive and they were so innocent, that is when she knew that she couldn't be a mother. Wasn't good enough for them. Couldn't give them anything at all they needed. She saw that they deserved everything, not some girl from the bush who didn't know anything about babies, who didn't have anything, not even her own home, no cribs, no baby clothes, nothing at all. She didn't work, she didn't have any way to support these two little boys who were so beautiful who would only be ashamed of her and who would only suffer at her hands. They wouldn't want her as a mother with her long scars down her arms, long, stringy hair, four year old runners, and who had no place to bring them to at all. They deserved a mother with a big house and lots of food and with fuzzy outfits to place them in, with soft hands, a quiet voice to sing to them with a father who loves them too.

Jolene couldn't breathe very well, was dizzy from the birth, sore and ashamed that she had nothing, was nothing, knew nothing about little lives so perfect and warm and soft. She stroked their hands and beeped the nurse with the gray hair and told her that she needed to talk to someone about adopting out these babies. She steeled herself and without tears and in a steady voice told the nurse to find the appropriate people to take the babies so they could be adopted out. She spoke to counselors, doctors, children's services and she watched herself from above while she spoke, wondering what she was saying, wondering why she looked so calm when all she heard was a wild wind whipping at her, beating her backwards like a tornado, down her throat, into her lungs, her spirit pulling it all in. She saw her hand lift and sign and watched herself just lie there, quiet, so slack, eyes firm on the two babies lying side by side, hands touching, their chests rising and falling like the break of day, so necessary and permanent.

Sweat

Lying beside them is like medicine. She dreams with them in her arms that she is in a nice home filled with pictures on the wall, and a rug filled with things the babies can play with. She sees a house long and wide that holds the three of them safely, where there is everything she needs to take care of them. Where there are arms everywhere to lift these boys and carry them. A big bed with a blue speckled quilt where she lies with them and talks to them and tells them about this journey and she is angry. She is so angry that she doesn't know how to get this vision activated. That nobody comes to claim them. That she will walk out with these boys and they will be watching here with those eyes and she has nothing at all to show them. She can't breathe. She has nowhere to take them. Please let me stay another day to lie with them. Just let me lie here while the world makes noises and families walk out with their babies in carseats and fuzzy blankets, when all I came here with is my body filled with life, and nothing else. I can't look them in the eyes. I am a windigo for forcing this life on them. I am the windigo mother with two perfect babies and my body trembles and pulls back. My body doesn't want to know them because their eyes might see that I have nothing am nothing but that dark wind that blew them into breathing.

And she left the babies three days later, walked out of the hospital without them, left the babies in the Plexiglas bassinettes, their little eyes shut so quietly, never knowing that she was leaving, her eyes on their faces, memorizing them, sending them the silent message that she loves them, she loves them, she loves them so very much, but she is not good enough, does not know enough, does not have enough for them. And she left them without looking back, her heart stuck so deeply in her throat that she was gasping for air by the time she reached the car, gasping for an air that was thick and foggy and so gray that it choked her with its presence, leaving her deadened, but moving, turning the wheel, pushing the pedal and leaving the hospital a brown speck in the background, her whole life left behind for the taking.

And now they have a chance without me.

But now she had found out where they were, so many years later, and she knew she had no right to them, but she wanted to see them, wanted to see their faces, the little faces she remembered and she wanted to see them smile and be happy and needed to see that they were alright. *She has no right to them, does she?* The question gnawed at her, chiseled itself out of her, and she felt little scrapings of her heart falling at her feet. *Does she? Does she?*

26

Beth

WHEN SHE FIRST WENT TO PICK UP THE BOYS, she was prepared. Two carseats, two cribs, two of absolutely everything. She bought and bought and her husband didn't say a word. But he watched her. Always watched her. She lined up everything together in the closet, blues and greens and yellows and creams all coordinated like a long palate, little sleeves and footsies floated together in the closet, smelling of fleece and baby powder. Her husband didn't speak, but he would come into the room and look around quietly before turning and making his way down the hallway to the bedroom, his socked feet padding slowly, sounding like rain against a mudpile, soft and thick.

She waited for their arrival as a mother waits for her baby in labour. She tried not to see a difference. Even though she was just being a foster mom to the twins that the agency told her about, they made it clear that their mother wanted nothing more to do with them and that she had agreed already that the boys could be adopted out. Beth was elated and knew, even before meeting the boys, that she wanted them, wanted to adopt them, wanted them to complete their family. She would wait the appropriate time and then take the appropriate steps. Her legs shook as she walked into the Family Service building. Her husband walked beside her, his breath a steady in and out as it always was, matching carseats in each hand.

The social worker came toward her and shook her hand. The paperwork had been done weeks ago and now she was here simply to take the babies to their new home. They chitchatted momentarily and soon two ladies came out with two small bundles in their arms. The boys were wrapped tightly in striped blankets, their faces identical, both sets of eyes closed; their breaths fell over her like a spring rain, warm and soothing and serene. Her fingers shook as one by one they were placed in her arms. Tears fell over her cheeks, down her neck and dripped onto the white and blue blankets. The boys did not stir; they slept so deeply that Beth felt herself relax along with them. She was their guardian, and soon to be their mama.

The ladies smiled at Beth and her husband as they placed the babies in the carseats, covered them with blankets and walked out the door. As soon as she left the building, she felt different. Like life had handed her another chance. Like the world just opened up in front of her and laid out a new life just for her. She felt so special and happy that she couldn't ever remember being depressed or hopeless. The world opened its arms and she stood with her face toward the two babies and she embraced it back, took a giant step forward and ran straight into the world, never being so happy. She would never let anyone take this away from her.

They drove away, dusk falling, and she heard a laughter

following her softly. Her husband looked over at her, surprised. It was then that she realized it had been so long since she'd laughed, that she hadn't at first realized it was coming out of her own mouth.

Now, years later, bathing them, feeding them, mothering them and loving them, she knows that they were meant to be her children, even if they didn't come out of her own body.

"Come on kids. There is a round dance happening at the Station Mall," Beth says to the children, both of them watching her. "You know, it's happening because of the Idle No More Revolution that is going on. Remember all the things we talked about?"

"You talk to us about all sorts of things." Keith rolls his eyes. "How can we remember just this one?" His voice echoes, little raindrops splitting the silence of a still night.

"I remember, Keith," says Juno. "Remember all the stuff that we are hearing about right now. Chief Spence isn't eating. Stephen Harper isn't listening. Remember Keith? The native people are standing up because of the broken...is it treaties mama?" Juno asks.

"Yes honey. The treaties. Remember we talked about these things when you had that history assignment about our prime ministers? Remember how I explained how there was a three way agreement that was not honoured between us native people, the government and the crown?"

"I know. And now we are standing up for our rights. Telling them we know that this trickery is happening, huh?" Juno's eyes are big.

"Isn't it too late anyways?" Keith asks. "So, why should we bother? Why should we even go anyways? I'd rather play with my new ipod."

"Because we have to care. We haven't cared long enough honey. We are going and we will have a good time." Beth grabs their hands and opens the door to a winter that places her breath onto their feet as they walk, places her whiteness into dancing around their journey.

The Station Mall holds her door open like an offering. It isn't hard to find the dancers, the sounds of drumbeats from center court resounding like a deep throbbing. Spectators, activists, participants and loud and beating hearts cut through the throng of daily activity. Beth sees people surrounding the dancers in curiosity, wondering where this is from and why it is here. The onlookers form a semi-barricade and the dancers continue, ancient and thriving, dozens of hands pressing against others, a collective energy that drives the motion.

"Look," Beth tells the boys, pulling their hands toward hers, mesmerized, wanting to pull the boys into the circling of swelling life.

"It's beautiful," Juno breathes.

"It's embarrassing," mutters Keith, restless feet shuffling.

"Let's go closer." Beth pulls them toward the sound of the dancers, the energy gnawing at her bone marrow, the hands braided together, the entwining of history reflected in this image of hands on hands, a twirling into the future.

They stand behind the circle of dancers, the round dance a drumbeat that reverberates into their chests, all hands seeming to be manifesting a never-ending circle. Beth pulls the boys closer, says, "Should we join the circle?"

"Let's go," says Juno.

"Let's just watch instead," says Keith, his feet kicking into each other.

"Let's just try it boys. Come on." Beth breathes excitedly, pulling both boys forward and finding hands to latch onto, to hold and to embed energies within. Beth holds her two sons' hands and watches as they hold hands and walk within the drumbeats of the movements. She watches their small feet catch the rhythms. She exhales when their feet hit the ground in synch with the other dancers. She doesn't care that some people are wearing moccasins and they are wearing runners and polished sandals.

This is not what this revolution is about. This is about something else. What is this thing that raises our people to a point that cuts history in half? This is the truth. Debwewin. Truth in motion.

They move round and round the circle of people, all connected, a pulsing of drumming making them feel like they could be anywhere, that they are dancing over the centre of the earth. A feeling of connection with her sons, and with all of the other people in the circle begins to grow in Beth's core, and tears heat the back of her eyelids with the recognition that she feels completely free and sure for the first time that she can remember. She looks over at Juno with his little mouth wide open in laughter, watching the movement's motions. Beth looks over at Keith's face and her heart brims over when she sees a smile on his face, his eyes lit up and his little body bouncing up and down with the rhythm of the drumbeats as he moves in the circle. She has never seen him so happy, has never seen his body dance before and she is spellbound by her son's movements, his effortless gliding to the power of the round dance. Beth looks at the woman beside Keith, her beautiful cheekbones and long neck, the way her long, dark hair falls down her back and moves like currents against her red t-shirt. There is a deep familiarity and she is sure that she has met this woman somewhere before in the community. She moves between feelings of love and joy in rapid succession.

When the round dance ends Beth is aware of the people in the mall, watching, joining the dancers, and feels there was a real sense of acceptance today from the non-Indigenous onlookers and sup-

151

porters. She holds her sons' hands and looks around at the energy, the tears, the laughter and the power of the Anishinaabe people today. The women looks beautiful in their long skirts and hand-drums. There are men, women, youth and even babies holding Idle No More signs. Her boys are in awe, looking around at everything, smiling and pointing out different things to each other.

"Look, Juno!" Keith shouts. "There's Billy from school and he's not even Native and he's holding a sign. This is pretty cool."

"Yeah!" Juno breathes. "Check out the eagle feather that man is holding. Awesome!"

They are all so busy looking around and searching the crowd that Beth doesn't hear the beautiful woman that was holding Keith's hand during the round dance approach them. She kneels beside the boys and looks deep into their faces. Beth watches, thinking she looks graceful.

"Miigwetch for holding my hand young man," she whispers.

"Geez, I don't know how to say 'you're welcome' in Ojibway or else I would," Keith responds.

"That's okay with me. My name is Jolene. What are your names?"

"I'm Juno and this is my brother Keith," states Juno, eager to talk to the pretty woman with dark eyes before them.

"Well, I am happy to see you both here today. That's for sure." The woman stands and continues to watch the boys, her lip shaking.

Beth watches as an older woman comes up to the woman Jolene and takes her by hand. The woman smiles at Beth.

"Hi, I'm Elsa. Wasn't this powerful today?"

"Absolutely," Beth smiles. "I am so glad that we came."

"Me too!" say Juno and Keith at the same time.

The three women look at the two boys, and laugh. The laughter carries downward, falls like rain over the boys' heads until they start laughing too. Elsa reaches over and grabs Beth's hand and Beth reaches over and grabs Jolene's hand, forming a tight circle around the boys, their laughter vibrating together under the fluorescent mall lights, through the throngs of people, and the energy of the movement, sounding like the bubbling of a brook, newly birthed.

27

The Grandmothers

THE FEAST LASTS FAR INTO THE NIGHT. The women's faces flicker beside the great fire. So many, gathered. Faces licked by the edge of shadow and light, fire sweating their features, suckling the cold of the evening from them, bit by bit. Furs drape over their shoulders, herbs hang, blowing softly inside the autumn wind, and scents of burdock and yarrow and nettle hang over them, softening the air, making it drip with their life. Some women sing, others drum, some cry from the beauty of the sound, small tears falling onto the earth which sucks them down hungrily, the thirst from its daughters satiating the grounds.

There are many women, together. Young women nursing their babies, small cheeks indenting in and out quietly, their breaths warming the flesh of their mothers, their hands resting softly on a breast, like a brush from a feather-tip or a long wisp of smoke edging into the spirit. Old women laying out the sturgeon, the flesh of the fish opened as a sacrifice, the flesh of the fish pinkened and smoky, hands settling the meat on the long platform of wafting foods, old hands with crevices as deep as history, as intertwined as the lives joined together. So many women, gathered, babies in all stages, so many women, their breaths making a chorus, a palate of colour and song.

They invite the animals who watch from the sidelines, and they come, step forth from the shadows, and the men move aside to allow their presence this night. They nibble on bones and flesh from the meat, small black eyes glimmered and blending with the others. A grandmother reaches down to stroke the stiff fur of the beaver, to thank him for his work on their rivers. A mother cradles an otter who has come forth and he accepts her touch, warming under her flesh. A daughter beckons the muskrat, who hesitates, and then moves toward her, to sit and join her in the journey of song and food and creation. He nudges the sleeping infants on her lap and the twins raise their heads and look at him. Smiling and tired, they sleep in the daughter's arms while an owl watches over them, while the eagle circles, while the men step forward to join the women.

Overhead, the sky opens and laughs. The grandmothers begin a slow laughter, the mothers look on, and the daughters sleep in the arms of the night with the babies, whose breaths are as steady and even as the whittle of an ancient hand, the quick falling of tree to earth, to soil. The fire blazes in the centre and from up above, it is a harvest of voices, lives, pain and endurance, and the sky rumbles its pleasure and sends its stars to accompany the feast, to blaze their glory over the gathered, and the whittling stops and the laughter carries on and on, all throughout the night, a low chorus that guides the birdsong, the rippling waters, and the mothers' hands as they lift the abundance to their mouths, and eat until their bellies are full.

Lesley Belleau

The night stills and the fire blazes, and all the women sleep, their bodies resting on thick furs beside the orange firelight, the moon heavy over them, full and round, watching over them, the babies, the mothers, the daughter, and the lone grandmother who sits alone, her hands holding the two infants so their mother can sleep, four small eyes closed softly, pale flesh covering them, her back against a great tree, its vast arms surrounding her, its bark burning against her back, bursting with a beating that keeps her awake, aware of her own heart like a drum beating within her. She sighs and takes the stillness and weaves it into her memory, over and over, like a swimmer curling long into the deep of the sea, aware only of the perfect purpose where the surface doesn't matter beside the place of birth, the thrust of recreation, the feel of water surrounding the flesh like a cocoon, a womb, a silent leaving of the body into the spirit, the falling of one life into another.

And the grandmother laughs for no reason at all, the whole world sleeping around her, and the two babies stir gently in her arms, the firelight playing on their features as they sleep, and she pulls them closer, small faces on her chest, sweat dripping onto her arm, and falling softly to the earth, a long teardrop, a drip that never ceases, a sound that lasts as long as time endures. The Grandmother looks above to the sky, a huge blackened length, and she finds what she is looking for at last, a pinprick of space in the sky and she knows that she is being watched over and cared for. *Gheezhigo-Quae, sleep,* she whispers to the night air.

And finally content, she too, sleeps.